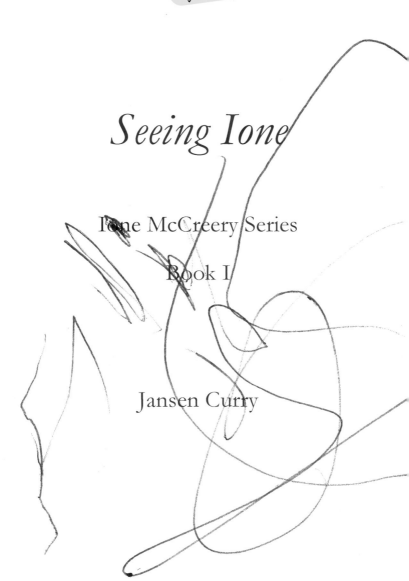

Seeing Ione

Ione McCreery Series

Book I

Jansen Curry

For S, K, and R

"Do what you feel to be right in your heart—for you'll be criticized anyway. You'll be damned if you do and damned if you don't." – Eleanor Roosevelt

ACKNOWLEDGMENTS

I have many people to thank. Mostly, I want to tell my husband and children thank you. Thank you for your faith in my desire to write, your patience, and most of all, thank you for your love.

I also want to thank all the people who encouraged me to write despite my own fear. Shannon Dutcher, you have been my editor, my cheerleader, and my friend through this entire project. I would never have seen this through without your help. To my parents, you have spent my entire lifetime telling me I can. Thank you.

Finally, I must give credit where it's due. I believe my desire to write the stories living in my head (however good or bad) is from above. I am grateful to God for this brutiful life. It is the best adventure.

Seeing Ione

ONE

April showers bring May flowers. What a load of crap. In Cattle Creek, spring was a wish. Angry wind cut through my sweatshirt as I made my way from the barn to the house.

"Hold on. I'm coming!"

The deliveryman stood in his truck erratically pressing the horn. I caught a glimpse of his face. He wasn't the usual guy.

"You can stop honking," I said, and turned to the house. "Beo. Go lay down." He didn't move. "*Bay-oh*! Go." The massive animal dropped his head and walked back to his favorite spot near the front door. "He doesn't recognize you."

"What kind of dog is that?"

1

"A wolf." I glanced at the man's expression, gauging if I was going to have to dive into an explanation. It wasn't legal in Wyoming to own a wolf, but the people in our staunchly conservative community of 460 souls used statewide laws more like general guidelines.

"Are you Ione McCreery? You don't look old enough to sign for legal docs."

"And you don't look smart enough to know the difference. You need to see my ID?"

Mr. UPS handed me his digital clipboard. I attempted a legible signature before he snagged it back and jumped into the truck to retrieve an envelope.

"Are you replacing the usual guy?" I asked.

"Covering while he's on vacation."

"Good."

He extended the package and lost no time pulling out of the drive.

I took a deep breath before pushing open the front door. Mingling smells of fried food and Copenhagen accompanied the mild glow of my dad's yellow-orange imprint that hung like a fog throughout the house. The emotions he felt most often left a residue in all his favorite places. An imprint engulfed his favorite leather chair. I hurried past the monstrosity as if it might bite me.

I slid into one of two mismatched chairs at my kitchen table and pushed my breakfast dishes out of the way. Beo sat on the floor next to me. His eyes studied my every move.

I pinched what was left of my uneaten bagel between my fingers and tossed it in the air. The wolf snapped his jaws, and the crusty leftovers vanished. He found a spot on the kitchen floor where the sun made its way through the window above the sink. Beo circled several times and lay down, soaking in the warmth of the sun. I envied his contentment.

The oblong design in the top left corner of the envelope was a stylized S&D for *Slade and Dyer Attorneys-at-Law*. It made my insides clench.

"Eff you, Slade and Dyer." I rubbed my stinging eyes.

The cover letter explained my father's estate was settled. More than sixty years of life and the only evidence was the deed for his family's 160-acre original homestead property, the title to a 1976 Ford F-250 pickup truck, and the key to a safe deposit box in Cheyenne. All of it was now in my name.

I tossed the stack of papers. The pile collided with a glass.

"Oh, come on!"

Beo jumped to his feet.

I grabbed the documents as droplets of water pooled on the floor. The papers were damp but salvageable. The small, blue envelope holding the key was ruined. I peeled away soggy paper and inspected the brass key.

Cheyenne was a two-hour drive from the ranch. In Big Red, my dad's old—*my* old–pickup, it would cost a small fortune in gas to get there. If the power steering went out again, I'd be up shit creek without a paddle. I was about as mechanically inclined as a sock monkey.

Knowing Bill McCreery, the box was full of sentimental keepsakes—nothing of immediate importance. But Jenny was heading that way in a few hours to visit her mom for the weekend.

I texted her and asked if I could catch a ride. While I waited for a reply, I cleaned up the mess I'd made. My phone buzzed. I read her response and released a sigh of equal parts relief and apprehension. New places could be a minefield of imprints. People painted the world with their emotions. Perhaps I was the only one who could see them, but they were always there—fogging my life.

I went upstairs to put a few things in a bag for an overnight stay. I grabbed a T-shirt, a clean pair of underwear and my bathroom kit—good enough.

The only thing I'd used in the bathroom in the last week was my toothbrush and the toilet. I caught a look at my self in the mirror. Staring back at me was a face I didn't recognize. Violet eyes that always drew attention gazed back haloed in dark circles. Long black hair hung lifeless and greasy in its tie at the nape of my neck. I leaned into the mirror.

"Jenny is going to kick your ass."

TWO

Semi-trucks flew by Jenny's compact sedan in a blur. Narrow gaps between trailers revealed only momentary glimpses of white snow and brown earth. The residue of winter still clung to the plains, giving no indication of the lush prairie that would connect Laramie to Cheyenne in two months time. For now, it appeared barren and cold. Not at all different from the ache in my chest.

"What's in the deposit box?" Jenny asked, as we approached the interstate off-ramp.

I shook my head and turned to her. "Bill-type treasures."

She laughed. "You mean antique Ford manuals and Johnny Cash cassettes?"

Jenny's wide grin lifted her cheeks, emphasizing sparkling green eyes. Mahogany spiral curls framed her face and setoff the sprinkling of freckles across her nose. We were opposites in so many ways.

"Thanks for the ride. Big Red isn't ideal transportation right now. I'm not sure she'd make it, and it would've cost my entire paycheck to pay for gas."

"It's a total pain in my ass." She couldn't keep a straight face.

"Thanks anyway."

There was a long pause. Jenny's jaw tightened. Her eyes left the road ahead to peer at my listless body in the passenger seat. I braced myself for a lecture.

"You missed the registration deadline for fall classes." She was careful not to sound too disappointed.

I shifted in my seat. Guilt lodged at my sternum. "I'm not ready to go back."

"You're not ready? *Whatever.*"

"What's that supposed to mean?"

"You're like a ghost trapped in that shithole of a house. It's been three months, almost four. I know this has been miserable and so freaking sad. But *you're* not dead. You know, you're lucky."

I narrowed my eyes.

"You said your goodbyes. He lived a good life. I'm not saying you have to forget or pretend you aren't still grieving, but you have to try for some kind of normal life. Nothing you can do will change what happened. He's not coming back."

I ground out a response through clenched teeth. "Yeah, I know."

Uncomfortable silence filled the car.

"It would hurt him to see you like this." Her voice had changed.

Guilt dropped from my throat into my gut. I closed my eyes and leaned into the window. Cold glass pressed against my cheek. If I focused on the cold, maybe the tears wouldn't come.

Jenny reached across the console and held my hand. The warm touch coaxed me out of my desire to implode into nothingness. I pulled away from the door and looked at our hands. Her pale fingers wrapped around mine. I could see a hint of the burn scars that covered most of her body.

When Jenny was a baby, a pressure cooker exploded in their kitchen. A grenade of scalding water liquefied the room. Jenny was sitting in an infant chair on the floor when it happened. The accident left her with second- and third-degree burns on most of her lower body and parts of her forearms.

The scars frightened me the first time I noticed them. That changed when I realized she felt different in much the same way I did. Her scars were now masked by the power of her personality and hidden under a decade of devoted friendship.

She still wore what was left of a tattered homemade bracelet I'd given her in the fifth grade. It emitted a bright tangerine imprint of deep affection.

"I hate when you're right," I said.

"You must hate me all the time." She took back her hand and flicked her bouncing curls behind her shoulder.

I sucked in a deep breath that lightened my body. "I won't promise you I'm going to go back to the university. But I can try to return to the land of the living."

"Hallelujah!" Jenny momentarily threw her hands up in mock praise.

A genuine laugh escaped my unguarded lips.

"I'll drop you off downtown. I've got to stop at my mom's office. Text me when you're ready."

She stopped the car in a fire zone.

I stepped out, gave her a wave, and watched the car pull away.

Plainsman National Bank was the tallest building in downtown Cheyenne. The new construction and reflective windows looked out of place among the other western-themed structures. I stepped through automatic double doors and was assaulted by heat from overhead vents. An old pegboard sign directed me to the safe deposit lockers upstairs. My boots scratched against the foyer's marble tile sending echoes through the empty stairwell.

A middle-aged woman with a helmet of blond hair and copious amounts of aqua eye shadow was perched behind a desk at the top of the stairs. She gave me a practiced smile. Blondie wasn't a fan of her job. The computer, desk, and phone were clouded in deep red. She'd imprinted a fair amount of anger. I ignored the glow and offered her a smile.

"I need to get into a safe deposit box."

"Well, ain't you a sweet treat. I'd give just about anything to have your skin tone, honey. Oh, heaven! And those eyes, they're lilac, ain't they? Wouldn't mind stealing an inch or two off you, neither." She winked.

When she said honey, it was thick and sweet as if she was trying to sound the way honey tastes. She wasn't from Wyoming. I was relieved to discover she was kind despite what her workstation indicated.

"Are you Indian?" She chomped on neon green gum like it was the only thing she'd eaten in a year.

Jenny called my skin tone *non-committal*. Most people in Wyoming assumed I was at least half Native American. Their guess was as good as mine.

"I'm sorry," she said, "that was probably rude. Is *Indian* not okay to say? Wait. Don't answer that. It's no matter, anyway. You're gorgeous whether you're Indian or alien." She stopped chomping and gave me her best apologetic smile, different from her practiced smile only because it was somehow more genuine.

9

"It's okay." I provided my own tight-lipped grin.

Her face relaxed. "I'll need to see your ID. We just want to keep a record of who's going in and out. What's the box number, sweetie?"

I dug into the bag hanging across my body and pulled out the key.

"Nine-one-one,"

Blondie laughed under her breath. I realized what I'd said and rolled my eyes. In all likelihood, my dad chose that number not to be ironic. It was one of only a few numbers he might remember.

"Follow me. Take your time, and when you're ready to go, just buzz. I'll come right back. Okey-dokey?"

I nodded my understanding.

We passed through a main door where Blondie punched in a security code. She gave me another wink as she strolled back to her desk. When I heard the security door click shut, I walked down the wide aisle of safe deposit boxes. Number 911 was at the end of the first row. I placed my key into the keyhole and turned. The door popped open. I pulled out a surprisingly heavy metal box and carried it to a small desk.

"Okay, Bill McCreery. What do you have for me?" Goose bumps tiptoed up my arms. I flipped the lid open and gasped. "*Holy shit!*" I cupped my hand over my mouth.

"Y'all-right in there, hun?" Blondie was standing at the security door.

I closed my eyes. "I'm fine. I'll be out in a minute."

Or whenever I recovered. I opened my eyes fully expecting to see I'd been hallucinating.

They were still there. Sitting inside the metal box were stacks and stacks of one hundred dollar bills. I picked up the first bunch. One hundred in each stack neatly tacked with paper and a rubber band. I'd never seen that much money in one place in my life. I wasn't sure I'd seen that much money *in my life*.

As I moved the stacks, I noticed something was glowing the telltale yellow color of Dad's emotional imprint——an envelope. I opened it carefully. I only had a handful of handwritten mementos from my dad. I was sure this one was going to be a keeper.

Ione,

I'm sorry for a lot of things, but I'm not sorry you're my daughter. I'm not sorry I took you in. I'm not sorry for a single moment of life I was able to spend with you. I'm not even sorry I let you keep that damn wolf.

I am sorry I haven't been honest with you about what I know of your past. I was asked to keep a secret so that you

11

were safe. I've decided I'll tell you what I know. Do with it what you wish.

Joanne Sloane was the person who brought you to my door more than a decade ago. She convinced me to take you in when she said you were a distant relative of my wife's. I never met Patty's family. She told me her family was part of a painful past. That was explanation enough for me. When she died, there were no cards or letters, no condolences from anyone outside of our small town.

Joanne and Patty shared everything. They'd been best friends for nearly forty years. When I asked Joanne where you'd come from, she reminded me of a promise I'd made to Patty. My wife asked me to swear I would always keep her secrets. It seemed a silly agreement between us, but it was something she made me repeat frequently. When Joanne brought it up that day, I knew you were a secret I had to keep.

Three days after you arrived, a man came to visit. He explained your family was associated with some kind of cult. He said your parents wished you to be kept outside the organization's reach. He offered me a deal.

If I kept you safely secluded in Cattle Creek, and allowed you to keep the gifts he'd brought for you—a wolf pup and a small hope chest, I would be provided with a financial gift from your family. It would cover the costs of raising you as well as allow me to keep my ranch from being foreclosed.

I would've cared for you no matter what. I'd promised Patty. I took the money to save the ranch. Maybe it was wrong. That makes no difference now. The ranch is yours along with the remainder of the money. You'll find the hope chest in the basement. I kept my end of the deal. I never heard from the man again.

Patty is gone, Joanne is gone, and I'm not long behind. I wish I had more to leave you than an old man's story and an empty house. Use the money to find what makes you happy and to hell with the rest.

Dad

I folded the letter, placed it on top of the cash, and closed the deposit box. I hid my face within the folds of my arms to muffle my sobs. Several minutes later, I wiped my tears with the hem of my T-shirt and pushed myself up.

I was unprepared to carry out the stacks of cash. I'd have to come back with a duffle bag. The absurdity of that fact hit me. I laughed out loud while tears continued to fall.

THREE

Beo turned his head back every twenty feet or so to be sure I was still behind him.

"Yeah…I'm coming." I exhaled the words in a cotton-mouthed whisper.

I was talking more to myself than to him. Too bad the giant wolf refused to wear a leash. Forget about pulling me. A little help up the hill would've been nice.

I'd made this run so many times I could do it blindfolded. I knew the exact distance of every incline stretch and where to bail off onto the shoulder to avoid loose gravel. Despite the fact that I had the route memorized in detail, the five miles never seemed to get easier. It was difficlut to push my body to be faster and stronger, but the release I experienced when I was finished was worth any temporary pain.

Growing up, I started running to tame the anxious energy always bubbling just below the surface of my skin. Since my dad's death, running was what kept my depression from eating me whole. I wanted to run as soon as I woke.

Today marked what would've been my eleventh year at the ranch with my dad. It was also my birthday. Well, according to Bill McCreery, it was my birthday. Since it was anyone's best guess as to the date of my birth, we decided to mark the anniversary of my arrival in Cattle Creek as my birthdate.

I had two choices—sulk about celebrating without my father, be slowly eaten by my depression, and never hear the end of it from Jenny. Or I could go for a run and try to outpace the darkness that was fighting to permanently settle into my bones.

The moment my feet crossed the invisible property line, I doubled over with my hands on my knees, and checked my GPS—5.01, 40:10:00.

"Damn it." I'd missed my goal by ten seconds. "I blame you, Beo." The enormous wolf tilted his head and pulled his panting tongue into his mouth.

I pinched the circular knob on the side of the display to check the time—7:45 AM. Jenny didn't get off work until 4:00 PM. I'd promised her I wouldn't be a hermit on my birthday. We'd made plans to make the short drive into Laramie for shopping, dinner, and a concert.

At the end of the summer, Jenny would begin the last semester of her teaching degree. After she finished her student teaching, she'd go wherever she could secure a job. I was guaranteed only a few more weeks with by best friend. Our days of being together were potentially numbered. Tonight was a legit excuse to act our age and revel in our freedom and current lack of responsibilities.

Although she was living in Cattle Creek volunteering over the summer before student teaching began in the fall, Jenny kept her apartment in Laramie. The small university town wasn't the big city. Even when school was in session, the population hovered around thirty thousand people. In comparison to Cattle Creek, it was a thriving metropolis. We'd pack in as much as we could tonight, but I had nine hours to fill.

I cleaned the kitchen, vacuumed the rest of the house, worked on a new playlist for our drive, and showered. I managed to waste more than an hour sifting through my closet desperate to put together an outfit that would meet Jenny's standards. I settled on denim capris and a black, satin tank top. It was a minimum-standards outfit, but my hair was clean and I'd put on mascara.

I checked my watch— 12:55 PM.

I scanned the house for something else to take up time. My eyes landed on the cherry wood hope

16

chest I'd brought up from the basement. I'd braved the clinging spider webs of the downstairs cellar to see what the mystery man left me. The trunk had an imprint—maroon, a color I'd never seen.

Something else was different about the imprint. Most hung like clouds of various densities around their objects. This imprint radiated in waves. I walked over to the chest and kneeled. I flipped up the lid. It was empty. Just as it was the first time I'd looked—weeks before.

I ran my hand along the inside corners and walls. Beo wandered into the room to supervise. He stuck his head into the coffer and sniffed, focusing on the left, rear corner. He scratched at one of the legs.

"Quit it." I batted at his paw.

There were no scratch marks where he'd made contact, but there was a strange imperfection at the bottom of the side panel. I ran my fingers along the grain. It felt different than the rest of the piece.

I carefully flipped the trunk on its back, exposing the underside to light. I could see a small square had been cut out and replaced with newer wood.

There was a tiny indentation at the center of the square. I put my index finger into the concave mark. It made a barely audible pop and what I'd thought was a patch, became a hidden compartment.

I could hear something rattling as I opened the drawer and realized it wasn't the chest that was imprinted. It was the ring hidden inside.

A purple stone set in gold shimmered in the sunlight. The band was thick and embellished with engraved symbols of some kind.

I studied the pulsing maroon imprint. I sensed nothing—no emotional sensations or indications. Every emotion had its own color. What the hell was maroon?

My computer screen caught my attention. I sat down and searched for any and every clue as to what a maroon imprint might mean. I read pages about auras, chakras, interior design, and color psychology. The information had no consistency. I'd never heard of anyone being able to see emotional imprints like me. Calling up a fellow "color seer" wasn't an option.

The symbols were also a mystery. I attempted the same detailed search for an alphabet that matched the markings on the ring. I found nothing.

My phone rang in the kitchen. I shot out of my room and leapt over the four steps leading to the main floor. The house shook as I pounded onto the floor. I grabbed my phone. It was Jenny.

"I'm going to be out of here early. Pick me up in twenty." She sounded elated to be done with work for the week.

"I'm on my way," I said.

"Ione?"

"Yeah?"

"*Happy birthday!*"

18

FOUR

Laramie was vacant of most students but alive with the excitement of long, summer nights and warm temperatures. The Big Horn Bar hadn't changed since I'd left college. It was a bit dark as far as bars go, which fit a place that featured a bullet hole in the main bar room mirror and a stuffed two-headed cow proudly hanging on the wall. There'd been so many fights over the years that large red imprints stained the dance floor in pools of emotional blood spills. The place gave me the creeps, but I could ignore bad mojo for a good band.

When we walked inside, the stale air transported me to keg parties with frat boys. Dim

19

lighting made it difficult to maneuver without constantly bumping into sweaty bodies. After what seemed hours of loitering, we found a table.

A couple of Jenny's friends from the education department stopped to talk. I was happy to sip on my soda and listen. I startled when I heard my name.

"Ione, happy birthday!" Lindsey Duvall shouted over blaring stereo music. She reminded me of the women painted on warplanes, a voluptuous brunette with retro hairpin curls and ruby lips.

"Thanks." I smiled at Lindsey and shot Jenny a nasty face. She'd promised not to tell anyone it was my birthday.

"I'm gonna buy you a shot. Whatcha want? Lemon drop or slippery nipple?"

"Neither," Jenny said before I had the chance to answer. "She doesn't drink."

"Really? Didn't tag you as the holy-roller type." Lindsey tilted her head, obviously confused as to why any legit Wyoming cowgirl wouldn't want to exercise her legal right on her twenty-first birthday.

Navigating a world full of color imprints was challenging enough. Blurred and slurred wasn't something I'd be adding to the mix.

"How about *I* buy *you* a drink, Linds?" Jenny asked, as she put her arm around the other girl and pointed them both to the bar. A few minutes later, Jenny returned to our table alone.

"I meant to ask you earlier, what's up with the new bling?" She pointed her head at my chest. The ring hung just above where my cleavage should've been—if I had any.

Both the imprint and the symbols on the ring made me hesitate to wear it on my hand. I'd wrestled with the absurdity of my paranoia, but imprints were funny things, and my intuition and the pulsing waves of color told me maroon was representative of a strong emotion. Torn between leaving it hidden and keeping it close, I elected to put it on a chain around my neck.

"It's from…my dad. He left it to me."

"Let me see." Jenny extended her hand. I reached to unclasp the chain. As I pulled it away from my body, a shiver ran through me.

Jenny held the ring close to her face scrutinizing the stone and then turned the band around in her fingers to inspect the engraving. "It's the real deal isn't it?" Her voice quieted from shouting over the music to just loud enough for me to hear.

I shrugged in response.

"You should take it to get checked out." She handed the ring and chain back to me, and warming relief brushed my skin. I clasped it around my neck. "Hey, I think they're about to start." She turned to face the stage. "You want to move closer?"

"Any closer and we'll have to dance."

"God forbid!" She forced a look of shock.

"You should consider theatre as a minor."

She stuck her tongue out in reply.

The band had everyone in the bar up and singing along within minutes. Stained imprints on the band instruments painted a rainbow of colors. A gossamer layer of brown enshrined the drum set. The drummer was lonely or often lonely when he played. My own loneliness reared inside and took my breath away.

I watched the people around me. They fit together like puzzle pieces. Each person was different but could somehow seamlessly connect into the right place. If there was a place I fit, I sure as hell didn't know where, or how, to find it.

My dad was the only person I'd ever told about my second sight. When the one person in the world who knew the real you died, it was as if the real you didn't exist anymore. Jenny knew I was different. She teased me about being psychic, but I'd never told her details.

A chill crawled up my skin. I glanced around the muggy bar room sure I was being watched. Everyone was focused on the band or in conversation with someone. I shook off the sensation by rubbing my arms. I searched for Jenny. She'd snuck away while I was lost in my thoughts. She was, of course, on the dance floor. I caught her attention to let her know I was going to be right back. She nodded acknowledgement, and I headed to the door.

Warm summer breeze helped to subdue my chill once outside. I washed myself with a deep breath, hoping to erase my depressing thoughts. My nose filled with the scents of blooming cotton trees and the fried tacos at Paco's Taco Shed down the block. All the drunks would congregate there after the bars closed for the night. I leaned against the brick wall of the Big Horn and looked across the street to where we'd parked.

Beo sat on guard in the cab of Big Red. His insistence on coming had forced me to drive the truck. It was a miracle the old beater made the trip. At least now I had money to have the mechanical issues repaired. My father would roll over in his grave if I even considered purchasing a new vehicle instead of fixing up Old Red.

Beo bobbed his head in question of why I was standing outside before resting his massive skull against the driver's side doorframe. He tucked his muzzle into the nook of his leg and slept. My wolf was lecturing me about being sulky on my birthday and clearly communicating he wanted nothing to do with me.

I laughed and gathered myself to return inside, a little more determined to have fun.

"You alright?" Jenny asked, almost taking me out when I stepped inside.

"Yeah. Just needed to check on Beo and get some air."

"You ready to dance?" She asked.

"You think you can keep up?"

Her eyebrows shot up. "Oh, now you're cocky!"

Jenny led us to a small open area in front of the band. I made a conscious effort to ignore any imprints and lost myself in the music. I was in a trance until a chest grazed my back. I turned to see who was so close.

He was my height, but where I was a lanky six feet, he was solid. Probably a wrestler—thick neck, bloated hands, and a barrel chest that met a tapered waist. His ears stood out against a shaved scalp.

"Sorry, I didn't mean to scare you. You two were having so much fun, I didn't think you'd mind if I joined in."

Jenny stepped in front of me. "We have boyfriends who would *really* mind. So thanks, but no thanks. Have a good night!" She turned, blocking him. He pretended not to be offended as he backed away, checking to be sure no one noticed the exchange.

"Do I get to meet this boyfriend of mine who minds?" I smiled at Jenny, trying to silently express my gratitude.

"He's hot. I'm jealous." She winked.

We sang and danced until the band took a break.

"I'm dying of thirst. You want anything?" Jenny asked, pointing at the bar.

"Water, thanks."

She disappeared into the mob of bodies. I found an open space against the wall and leaned in. I fanned myself trying to lessen the sweltering effect of amplifiers, flashing lights, and the overwhelming lack of air.

"I don't think I've seen you here before?" I jumped. The same guy from the dance floor had me cornered. "I'd remember you." He smiled.

His face softened into something less intimidating when he grinned, but I felt no better about being cornered.

"I don't come here much."

"They're pretty good." He pointed to the stage. I forced a smile and nodded in agreement. "We're having a party at our place after this, if you and your friend want to come?"

"We're leaving when the band if finished. Thanks though." I glanced behind him.

"It's loud in here. Let's go outside and talk." His face was now so close to mine I could smell the whiskey on this breath. If the stench didn't make bile rise in my throat, the idea of being alone with him would.

"I'm waiting for my friend." I searched the bar again.

"No, really, let's go outside." He grabbed my arm to lead me.

I pulled back. "Don't touch me!" I hadn't meant to yell, but he made me anxious.

"Hey! Don't bother her!" Jenny shouted. She stood next to me.

The people around us grew quiet.

25

"I'm not bothering her. I barely touched her! I invited you two to our party, but on second thought, I don't think that's a good idea. We don't need any crazy-ass bitches ruining a good time." He spat the words as he leaned in close to Jenny's face. "You were a pity invite anyway." He deliberately looked at Jenny's feet. She was wearing cut-off denim shorts and sandals. Her burns were clearly visible. He contorted his face, showing his disgust.

Jenny put her head down in embarrassment. Anger lit inside of me like a gas fire. Before I could react, Jenny flipped her head back up. In one swift movement, she tossed the water she was holding into his face, grabbed his shoulders, and pulled him toward her as she drove her knee into his groin. He doubled over and began to gasp for breath before falling to the ground.

"I don't need, nor do I want, your fucking pity, you worthless piece of shit!" Jenny grabbed my hand and led us out of the bar. I heard mild applause and several masculine groans of sympathy as we walked out.

I put Beo in the bed of the truck. Jenny and I sat in the cab in silence for several moments. We both simultaneously broke out in hysterics.

"You are such a badass." I forced out the words in between fits of hilarity.

"I'm so sorry. That is *not* how I wanted your birthday to end." I realized her laughs had turned into quiet tears. My face flushed hot with anger as I thought of how his hateful words must have made her feel.

"I had a blast. And if you're upset about what that Grade-A douchebag said, don't be. You know better."

"You're right." She wiped away her tears. "Besides, he'll be thinking about me for a few days."

"Jenny, he'll be lucky if things are back to normal in a year." We both laughed. "You are always saving my ass. I love you, girlie."

"Awe, I love you too. Happy birthday, my sister from another mister." She gave me a crushing squeeze. Her hair smelled like coconuts and lavender. It almost overpowered the lingering smell of The Big Horn—almost. She pulled away. "Okay, let's go to my place. I think the Big Horn has had all of us it can handle."

"Agreed."

I fired up Red. As we pulled out of the parking lot in the direction of the apartment, another chill ran through my body. I braked and scanned the area.

"What?" Jenny knew something was up.

"Just…hold on." I kept surveying the street. Then I saw him, a glimpse of a man moving in the alley behind the bar. "There! You see that guy?" I pointed to the alleyway beyond the passenger side of the truck.

"Ione, look!"

The narrow gap of space between The Big Horn and the building next door was dark, but the two shadows were unmistakable. Light that fought to illuminate the alley lit up the face of the asshole who cornered me in the bar. Another, much larger man, was holding him against the side of the building.

"He deserves whatever he gets." I slammed on the gas peeling out my back tires.

"I told him you have a boyfriend who would mind," Jenny said, her voice giving life to the justification I knew we both felt.

FIVE

"I'm sorry." The pot-bellied and balding Mr. Alavaro, shook his head. I'd taken a shot at finding out more about the ring by popping into his jewelry shop in downtown Laramie. "You should send it to a lab. I'm a jeweler. I can't identify species outside of the range of what you see here." He gestured to the display case between us.

His tiny shop was blindingly bright with all the lighting used to make his jewels sparkle. I was out of place in a room where the merchandise in one display case was worth more than my house.

I slumped. "How long will a lab analysis take?"

29

"I'm not sure. Appraisal Associates in Cherry Creek is probably your best bet. You need an appointment. You can call and see if they have time tomorrow."

He inspected the stone through the magnifying eyepiece attached to his left eye. "Sure is a pretty setting for that cushion-cut stone. The engraving is unique. Wish I could help you more, but it's just beyond what I can do here in my shop."

"What else can you tell me?" I pushed.

"It's set in 24-karat yellow gold. The stone is approximately a half carat. It's old—possibly very old. But you'll have to have the lab determine the exact age." He pursed his lips together and sighed. "I believe it's an alexandrite—don't quote me. It has a number of the properties. The color shifts under my incandescent lights. That's almost a dead giveaway." The man paused again. "I just can't be sure." He looked up. "It needs to be tested."

Mr. Alavaro moved from behind his display counter and handed me the ring.

"I'll look into Appraisal Associates. Thank you." I looped my chain through the ring and clasped it behind my neck. The ring rested at the center of my sternum just above the open zipper of my jacket. I tucked the ring under my shirt and zipped my coat just to be safe.

"You should keep that someplace else. I'm sure the ring is quite valuable." Something jingled in his pocket as he nervously tapped one foot. "I wouldn't trust a thin gold chain." He turned and walked into an office marked PRIVATE.

I showed myself out. A gust of wind blew a handful of leaves in a race across the parking lot. A chill took me by surprise. I folded my arms, pulling my running jacket tighter around my shoulders.

A quick search for Appraisal Associates in Cherry Creek on my phone pulled up the number. A recorded message picked up. They were closed. I shoved my phone in my pocket and hoisted my body into Big Red. Beo sat erect in the passenger seat as if human and watched the passing vehicles.

The engine roared to life, filling the cab with the burning dust smell of transmission fluid. I said a quick prayer she would chug to Cattle Creek without problems. I needed to make one more stop before Jenny and I could head home. I hadn't quit my job at Circle R Seed N' Feed and was scheduled to work an evening shift.

I worked at the local feed store through high school. It seemed natural to go back when I moved home to take care of my dad. It was a predictable and physical job, and I was allowed to bring Beo to the warehouse. Taking more shifts was part of my return to the living I'd promised Jenny.

I parked outside Slade and Dyer Law Firm. Before my keys were out of the ignition, Beo growled.

A man stood at the far side of the parking lot. Something about him was familiar. I couldn't place where I'd seen him. While I continued to stare, anxiety drummed in my belly.

Mr. Creepers was propped against a light pole checking his phone. He wasn't creepy looking in a vagabond, obviously on drugs and dangerous, kind of way. Actually, he wasn't creepy *looking* at all— exceptionally tall, broad shoulders, muscled arms that forced shirtsleeves to stretch. Blond hair brushed his forehead, not long enough to cover his eyes. He wore a pair of faded jeans and black steel-toed boots.

It was clear the guy was attractive. With a build like his, as long as he didn't resemble Chewbacca from his chin to his eyebrows, he was what Jenny would call a Venti—extremely tall and hot.

Mr. Creepers was yummy. Unfortunately, he was a stranger standing in a parking lot, who, despite being attractive, was somehow setting off alarm bells. I dug out my phone and called Jenny.

"What did he say about the ring?" She asked.

"Nothing. It was a waste of time. I'm going to have to go to Denver and take it to a lab. Hey—I'm at my last stop. I'm being paranoid, but I'm picking up a creep-o vibe from this guy in the parking lot."

"Do you need me to come rescue you? It will take me at least half an hour to walk downtown." I could *hear* her roll her eyes.

"No. Just talk me off the cliff."

"Okay. How old is he?"

"I'm guessing our age, maybe a little older?"

"Is he hot?"

"Seriously?"

I heard her huff. "You have Beo with you, right?" She laughed as she asked.

"Yeah."

"You'll be fine. Remember when you called me convinced there was a ghost in the warehouse at the Seed N' Feed? Don't make me remind you about what happened after we watched that movie about the kids in the woods." She snorted. "No one's going to attack you in the middle of the day in a public parking lot. And *no one* is crazy enough to try and get at you with Beo on duty. That poor stranger—he has no idea you've turned him into a murderous psycho."

"Nobody can make me feel quite as stupid as you can." I unintentionally made eye contact with Mr. Creepers. I didn't listen to whatever Jenny was saying. I was too focused on keeping myself from drooling.

Creepers had light eyes contrasted by dark stubble growing over most of the bottom half of his well put-together face. His eyes locked on mine. Warmth rushed from the center of my torso down. A tingling sensation had me adjusting my weight in my seat. I realized how stupid I probably looked and glanced around the cab, pretending I hadn't been caught staring.

I tuned in to catch the last of what Jenny said. "—so I ended up volunteering. It'll all work out, but I have to stay in Laramie tonight. I can catch a ride back with Lindsay tomorrow. She's headed to Medicine Bow and can drop me off. You understand, right?

"Yeah, sure. I get it. Jenny…" My throat was suddenly dry. "Your question?" I swallowed. "Yes. Mr. Creepers is hot." I ended the call.

Beo stopped growling but continued to watch the man. "It's okay, boy." I grabbed the document for my attorney and slid out of the truck.

When I left the law office, the man was gone. I couldn't help thinking he would pop up any moment. I spent more time looking in the rearview mirror than watching the road in front of me on the drive home. More exhausting was the back and forth going on in my head. Yes, he kind of creeped me out—sort of, but I'd also hoped to see him when I'd left the law office.

I went into work early and pushed myself physically. I was about halfway through my shift when I slowed down enough to notice the extent of my exhaustion.

Jackson came into the warehouse to check my progress. The wiry man was a real-life cowboy cliché. I was easily six inches taller than my boss. My muscular frame, while slender, made Jackson appear petite. His size was deceptive. I'd seen him complete an eight second ride on an enraged two-ton bull as if it was a quick twirl on a carousel.

"Looks like you're almost done with that load. You want to come inside and run the register for a while?" He flashed a lopsided smile that showcased matching dimples and deeply set brown eyes.

"Actually, I'd like to take my break after I finish this."

He looked at his watch. "You getting sick?"

"Just tired." I gave him a weak smile and started stacking more bags of alfalfa cubes.

"No problem." He turned, heading back into the store. "You let me know if you aren't feeling good."

It was out of character for me to ask for an early break, but I was beat. I told myself the running I'd been doing was to blame, but I knew that wasn't true. I'd been tired for months.

Sleeping for hours on end started just after my dad died and continued into the months that followed. Though I'd been doing better the last several weeks, my energy level still didn't seem right.

I heaved the last two bags on the pile with a grunt and walked outside to check on Beo. He'd left the warehouse at some point. It wasn't like him to stay away long.

Crickets and frogs provided a soundtrack for an unusually still night. Gravel crunched under my boots, the sound reverberating in my body with each step. I didn't see him near my truck. I scanned the dirt parking lot. He wasn't within sight.

"Beo!" I called. Nothing. "*Bay-oh!*" I shouted again before walking through the employee entrance of the main storefront.

Everyone in Cattle Creek knew about my pet wolf. When Beo first showed up at the ranch, there was resistance—even anger. The wolf debate in Wyoming is a hot issue. People tolerated him because he'd never been caught misbehaving. The moment he was in the wrong place at the wrong time, he'd be shot. My pulse pounded in my ears.

"Hey Jackson, have you seen Beo?" I hollered.

"Yeah, he's in here."

I heard Jackson speak to a customer.

As I approached the counter, I caught a glimpse of Beo standing stock-still with his eyes locked on whoever was opposite Jackson. I scuffed my feet against the floor and stopped dead in my tracks.

A hot flush made its way to my cheeks, and I knew the swift body chill was coming before it crept up my arms and down my spine. Mr. Creepers was in Cattle Creek at the Circle R Seed N' Feed.

SIX

"I think this man is looking for you." Jackson raised his eyebrows.

"I'm sorry to bother you at work." Mr. Creepers gave an apologetic glance, first to Jackson and then to me. "I'm trying to locate a piece of antique jewelry. I was told a woman named Ione McCreery might have what I'm looking for?" He had a smooth, deep voice that fit his appearance and was dressed in clothing similar to what he'd worn before, only now he wore a black, leather jacket.

He stared at me expectantly. I realized I still hadn't said anything.

"I'm sorry. I didn't catch your name?"

He grinned. An even row of perfect white teeth exposed themselves from under full lips. His smile made me feel drugged. "Adric Silverman."

So, Mr. Creepers was really Adric Silverman. That was an improvement.

"What is it you're looking for?"

"A family heirloom…a ring to be specific."

The tops of my ears were suddenly hot. His body language was relaxed, arms casually resting with hands in his jacket pockets, but his gaze was intense.

Something about the situation made me nervous. It wasn't just that I was standing in front of one of the most attractive men I'd ever seen. While I should've been suspicious about having seen him in Laramie, that wasn't it either. There was something *else* about him that had me on edge.

"If you leave your phone number, I'll call you when I have time to talk."

Without breaking eye contact, he pulled out his wallet and extended a white business card. Beo growled.

"It's okay, boy." I patted his shoulder and stepped forward to take the card. I caught a whiff of leather mixed with a spice-like scent—cloves. An image of tangled sheets and sweaty bodies flashed trough my mind. I blinked, trying to jar the image from my head.

"A wolf is an interesting choice of pet." He looked at Beo with curiosity, but it was obvious he wasn't the least bit scared.

"Most people assume he's a dog."

"Most people see what they want to see."

Before I could respond, Adric Silverman was through the door. I turned the card over in my hand. It had no name, just a ten-digit number including an area code I didn't recognize. I slid it into my pocket.

"You sure you're feeling okay?" Jackson asked.

I leaned against the counter ignoring his question. "What do you think of that guy?"

"Typical big city. Waves his money and thinks he can get what he wants. What kind of name is Adric?"

"I'm not one to judge names." I half grinned at Jackson. He smiled back, flashing dimples. My anxiety settled some when I looked at his familiar face.

"He must really want what he's after if he went to all the trouble of hunting you down." Jackson's choice of words made something inside me flinch.

The rest of my shift dragged by. Jackson forced me to leave an hour early, telling me to go home and rest. He was sure I was coming down with something.

At home, I sat at the table, twirling Adric Silverman's card between my fingers. I pulled the ring out from under my shirt, unclasped the chain, and inspected it. The imprint was still strong. Even under the dim lights of my kitchen, the stone gleamed.

At first glance, the ring seemed too small for me to wear, but I hadn't tried. The band squeezed across the knuckle and came to sit comfortably at the base of my right ring finger. I let out a breath I hadn't realized I was holding.

I spread my fingers apart and reached my arm away from my body. The ring somehow made me feel a little prettier all over. It was heavier on my hand than I expected. The markings along the band were more visible than they'd been minutes before, and the imprint seemed to have weakened. I let out a heavy sigh.

I picked up the phone and dialed.

"Hello?" Adric Silverman's voice had the same smooth texture and deep tone.

"Is this…is this…Adric Silverman?" I sounded like a twelve-year-old girl.

"Who is this?"

I momentarily forgot my name. "Uh…Ione McCreery, from the feed store? Mr. Silverman, what can you tell me about the ring you're looking for?"

"I'd simply like to buy it. Name your price."

I was shocked by his directness. "I never said I had it."

His laugh rumbled in my ear. It had an unexpected raspy quality. Warmth began to grow just under my rib cage and crept outward.

"No. I guess you didn't." His laughter stopped. "But you did have it earlier today at Alavaro's jewelry shop."

I went stiff.

"It's bad luck. I'm doing you a favor. I'll pay you for it, more than you're likely to get anywhere else." His voice dropped to a tone that made me shiver. "I need the ring, Ms. McCreery."

It wasn't a coincidence I'd seen him in Laramie. He'd been following me. My stomach began to somersault. "It's not for sale." I paused to stoke my courage. "What do you know about the ring?"

"It would be better to talk in person."

"You can talk to me on the phone, or not at all." Adric Silverman radiated sex, but he also scared the crap out of me.

"You should be careful who you talk to about the ring." His voice dropped again, this time to a warning. The effect on me was equal parts turned-on and scared shitless.

"If you aren't going to tell me anything useful, we're done here. Although I'm sure the police will be more than happy to continue this conversation."

"You don't understand. It isn't safe for you to keep it."

Pain in my jaw told me I was clenching my teeth. I could hear blood making a *woosh-woosh* echo as it pounded through my head. "Stay away from me. If I see or hear from you again, I'll call the police…again, because I'll be calling them for the first time as soon as I hang up the phone."

He said something else I didn't hear. Making good on my threat, I dialed the sheriff's office and reported the bizarre exchange.

I thought about calling Jenny, but if I called her, she'd for sure figure out a way to drive back to Cattle Creek. Late at night she risked falling asleep or hitting wildlife.

I made my way around the house, locking all the windows and triple-checking the door locks. Afterward, I found myself standing in the doorway to my dad's darkened bedroom. The full moon beamed a spotlight through the curtainless window.

"Damn you, Dad." I rested against the doorframe.

He was supposed to be here. I was alone in his dilapidated house without anyone to tell me everything was going to be fine—that even though a strange man was following me, everything was going to be okay.

I walked into his room and stood in front of the dresser. Pulling open the top drawer, I caught a whiff of the sharp scent of Copenhagen Long Cut. My anger ebbed as the all-too-familiar hollowing pain of grief replaced it. I held my breath.

I pulled out everything as fast as I could, tossing socks and handkerchiefs over my shoulder. Unable to hold out any longer, I sucked in a deep breath. My father's smell filled my nostrils and poured into my lungs. The prickling of tears gathered at the back of my eye sockets.

"Come on…where is it?" My voice was strained with the emotion I was biting back.

The drawer was nearly empty when my fingertips touched cool metal, and I heard the thunk of the gun as I accidently pushed it farther into the drawer. I wrapped my fingers around the butt of the Colt .380 Mustang handgun.

I cradled it in my palm and angled myself in the moonlight to allow for a better view. I released the magazine cartridge and wasn't at all surprised to see it was full. I shoved the magazine back into place and walked to the bed.

A raised circular watermark on the nightstand caught a sliver of moonlight. Near the end, he'd been thirsty all the time. My memory replayed images of his glistening forehead, pasty face, and weakening body. I bit my tongue to distract from the building pain in my chest.

Next to the watermark, a picture of the two of us at my high school graduation sat in a cheap plastic frame. We both looked goofy in the slightly unfocused snap shot. My dad with his cowboy hat tilted, so there wouldn't be a shadow on his face, and me with my cap and gown in a hideous shade of baby food green. The photograph was imprinted—yellow, like all the things my dad loved. The picture was taken more than three years ago. A lifetime had passed since I'd graduated from high school. I bit down harder on the fleshy meat of the side of my tongue.

I set the gun on the nightstand and took in the sight of his queen-sized bed. A hand-stitched blue-and-white patchwork quilt Patty made covered the mattress.

Patty died in a car wreck fifteen years before I made my way into Bill McCreery's life. I'd never seen a single photograph of her. He said after she died, he just couldn't look at her picture. Now, as the image of the two of us carved a hole in my heart, I began to understand.

I slid my hands over the soft cotton of the quilt and pulled back the bedding. I was confronted again with my father's scent. Instead of fighting it, I crawled into the bed and buried my face into his pillow, drawing in as much of his smell as possible. I imagined the air filling the empty space inside of me. The mattress gave way as Beo jumped on the bed and lay down next to me.

"Let's sleep here tonight." I ran my fingers over his head and the soft hair covering his ears. Closing my eyes, I gave way to the sleep that was ready to take me.

SEVEN

"What a rip-off! You're not going to pay them, are you?"

I silently counted to three. "I agreed to pay the fee before they sent it to the Gubelin lab."

"But it doesn't tell you squat. What are you paying for?"

"Jenny, drop it."

I handed the woman behind the desk a certified check and fought nausea as she wrote up a receipt. I was as appalled as Jenny, but I'd agreed to pay the five-thousand-dollar fee for the comprehensive analysis before they sent the ring to

Switzerland. Of course, I'd done so thinking it would tell me more about the ring—a lot more.

I'd already spent several hundred dollars at Appraisal Associates in exchange for nothing more than more confusion. Learning about the ring was officially more expensive than my first semester of college.

I'd blown through almost eight grand to have the ring assessed and analyzed. I'd dumped another three thousand into fixing up Red. At this rate, I'd burn through my dad's money long before I got around to finishing school or anything else worthwhile.

"Excuse me…Amber, is it? What your company did here, it should be illegal." Jenny glared at the receptionist.

Undeterred, the woman handed me my receipt, the ring, and a packet of papers with the information accumulated from the analysis. I put the ring on and felt a missing part of me click into place.

The packet was a twenty-page report of chemical compound structure drawings and mumbo-jumbo I couldn't read. One of the gemologists at Appraisal Associates translated for me. I'd learned the ring was comprised of an alexandrite rock, from what region on Earth they didn't know. The 24-karat gold band was estimated to be approximately two hundred years old with engraving believed to be crude Hebrew symbols. That was it. The *expert* told me he'd never seen a piece come back with so little information from the Gubelin lab. Lucky me.

"Jenny." I grabbed her arm and pulled her from the counter. "Enough."

She reluctantly followed me through the door and we stumbled into the parking lot.

"I can't believe that just happened," she said, jerking away from me.

"What? That you just acted like a real housewife of…pick a city. Or that Amber, the front counter girl who doesn't have anything to do with the lab, didn't care?"

"Ione, why are you acting like this isn't a big deal? You just dropped five grand!"

"Lecturing the counter girl doesn't tell me anything about the ring, and it doesn't change the fact that I spent the money."

"You are so freaking stubborn. They're taking advantage of you. Five grand, Ione!"

"*I'm* stubborn?" I closed my eyes and forced my breathing to slow. "I have an idea."

"About how to get your money back?"

"No," I said, whispering it under my breath.

"You're going to call him."

I kept walking. "I have to. I can't explain it. I need to figure this out." I had to. Something had changed since I began wearing the ring.

In the month I'd spent wearing it, I could feel and perceive things in a new way. It wasn't just imprint colors I was seeing now. I could see and feel everything everyone around me was feeling.

The new dynamic was deeply intimate, allowing for a connection to people I'd been missing. The change was a challenge to navigate, but it felt *right*.

I wanted to tell Jenny about why the ring was so important to me, but it would mean telling her everything. I didn't want to admit I'd been hiding a part of me for the entire length of our friendship.

"You've gone off the deep end, sister. I get that it might be some kind of connection to your biological family, but let's be done with the ridiculously expensive wild goose chase. Let's *not* call the guy you reported to the police." Jenny crawled into the cab of my truck. I did the same.

"Just…trust me. The ring is the link. It has to be because…it's all I have." My stomach was in knots.

She shook her head. "I do trust you. I just don't want you to do anything stupid. Scratch that, anything *more* stupid."

"I won't." My intestines twisted again.

Twenty-six hours later, I sat alone at a corner café outdoor table in Laramie and fidgeted with my ponytail. Beo was lying beside me. It was late and past the season for eating outdoors, but the waitress said as along as I sat outside, my dog was welcome.

I ran my fingers through Beo's hair. He jumped up and focused on the door leading inside the restaurant. I soaked in the impressive sight that is Adric Silverman.

A now familiar sensation made its way through my body. It was no longer a chill of alarm but a buzz of anticipation. The difference was not lost on me.

Adric wore jeans, boots, and a white T-shirt under his black leather jacket. He moved with an athletic grace that distracted from the obvious strength his huge body possessed. As he sat, I intercepted his emotional energy—calm, but there was another emotion intertwined. I tried to focus and pinpoint what it might be. He smiled, and my brain tripped.

"I hope you weren't waiting too long." It was the fourth time I'd heard his voice, but I was still taken back.

"I have questions."

"Would you like to order something first?"

His blue eyes drilled into me. They were the same color as the Wyoming skyline; a blue so piercing it was almost unreal.

I'd spent much of my life perfecting my ability to blend in. I'd learned it wasn't hard to go unnoticed. When Adric looked at me, he gave me his full attention. I was the opposite of unnoticed. I realized he was also studying *my* eyes, and I broke our connection.

"I'm just having lemonade."

He gestured to the hovering waitress who'd been lingering in the doorway since his arrival.

"Can I get you something?" she asked, on the verge of panting.

"A pitcher of lemonade, please." The waitress scurried away and within seconds carried over a pitcher. Adric pulled out his wallet.

A bad perfume of nervous energy wafted off the waitress. Judging by her emotions, she was about to pass out…or orgasm. I was hoping for the former. He handed her a fifty-dollar bill.

"Thank you. We won't need anything else. You can keep the change."

"Oh? Are you sure? It's no problem." Her disappointment was palpable. I rolled my eyes.

"Yes." Adric was talking to her, but staring at me. The waitress left. "You said you have questions?" He leaned back in his seat and looked at Beo. The big wolf sat at my side focused on Adric's every move.

"I want to know about the ring."

He leaned in, resting his elbows on the table. His emotions shifted. Before I could determine what I felt, he masked the new emotion.

"How are you doing that?"

"Excuse me?" His body froze.

"Guarding—something like that. I can't read you. You're doing it on purpose, or at least I think you are." As soon as I said it, I wished I could reach out and pull the words back into my mouth.

His emotions changed again. I took a startled breath as a jolt of his excitement hit me. Beo stood and warned Adric with a growl.

"A Seer." The astonished whisper from Adric was automatic. He'd said it out loud, but he wasn't speaking to me. He put up his shield again. As suddenly as I was hit, the emotion was gone. I could breathe again. His emotions were much stronger than anyone else I'd been around.

"What did you call me?" He wasn't listening. "Adric?"

"We should go. We have more we should talk about but not here."

"You're bat-shit crazy if you think I'm going anywhere with you. I won't follow suit with the waitress and do as you say just because you flash your dreamy smile. In fact, I think we're done here. I've already said things I wish I hadn't." I stood to leave.

"Wait. We can stay here if that makes you more comfortable. We need to talk." He glanced around the patio. He seemed sincere, which made me conflicted—a theme when he was around.

"When I asked you about guarding your emotions, you understood?"

"Yes."

I sat. Beo followed suit.

"How did you find the ring?" His voice was barely above a whisper.

"It was a gift."

He nodded. "But it was hidden somewhere until recently." He searched my face. "Where?"

"In a hope chest."

He leaned into the table. "And, how did *you* find it?"

I knew what he was asking. I hadn't told anyone other than my dad about my color sight. It felt like a betrayal to tell Adric before Jenny. For reasons I couldn't explain, Adric seemed to understand without my telling him anything.

"The ring has its own emotional imprint." I closed my eyes and willed myself to explain. "I followed the colorcast. It was hidden in the hope chest in a secret drawer."

I anticipated an expression of confusion or disbelief, but when I made eye contact, he only appeared engaged in what I was saying.

"I want to be sure I understand." He leaned in closer. "You didn't sense the ring? You actually saw something that led you to it?" He was genuinely curious about the details.

"It was casting an imprint color I'd never seen before—a shade of maroon. I usually only see mild variations of eight colors. Maroon isn't one of them." I waited for his response. Each moment of silence made the pounding of my heart echo in my head.

"And just now, you said you couldn't read me."

"People are different. Things and places have colors." I swallowed and shook my head. "That doesn't make sense. Let me start over."

Adric reached across the table and placed his hand on mine. "Take your time." I glanced up and was met with a blast of calm emotion.

I started again. "I have a limited memory of my childhood, but as far as I know, I've always been able to see what I call emotional imprints. Color casts, similar to auras I think, they're like a residue left behind on objects and places when someone has an intense emotional connection. After I started wearing the ring, I could interpret other people's emotions too. Instead of just seeing colors, now I can *feel* the emotions. It's unnerving, but it seems like it's *right*." I paused to swallow. "I sound like a complete nut job."

He smiled and ran his thumb back and forth across the back of my hand. A tantalizing chill ran up my spine. I took my hand back.

Adric didn't say anything. I needed to fill the quiet. "This is where you tell me all about the ring and answer my unspoken questions."

Beo jumped to his feet. Before I could process what was happening, he was off like a shot.

EIGHT

"We need to leave. You're coming with me." Adric stood next to me. I stared at him, stunned. "You'll have to trust me." He placed a hand on my elbow and directed me to the street.

"Hold on. I've got to find Beo. Someone might figure out he's a wolf, and if they don't shoot him on sight, the Game and Fish will."

My heart hammered in my chest. Beo never ran off. He rarely left my side, even for a moment. A full-on runaway just didn't happen.

"Your wolf will be fine. He'll find you. Trust me." Adric grasped my elbow again.

I pulled back. "I *don't* trust you. Why should I?"

"Read me. What's my intention?" Adric stared, waiting for me to do something.

"I can do that?"

For the first time in our very unusual conversation, he looked at me like I was crazy. "Just try it."

I attempted to calm down and clear my head. After I sifted through my emotions and identified his, I dug deeper. Beyond the layers of feelings, just past his guarded calmness, I found what I was searching for.

"Why do you want to protect me? You don't even know me."

"Trust it. We need to go. Beo will find us." He pulled me by my arm a third time, and this time I followed.

"How do I know you aren't…I don't know…mind-lying?" I took a step backward.

Adric inhaled, expanding his deep chest, and I sensed his growing desire to leave the restaurant. "Do you know who you are?"

There was something in the way he said it. He wasn't asking me if I knew. He was telling me that *he* knew. "What the hell is going on?"

"I can tell you. And I can tell you more about the ring, but not here. I want to talk to you somewhere…" he paused, "…else." I had the sinking suspicion he'd carefully chosen the word *else* instead of the word *safe*. "Your wolf will find us. We aren't going far." Adric walked to a black Mercedes Coupe parked outside the restaurant and opened the passenger side door. "I've rented a cabin outside of Woods Landing. It's a better location."

It was stupid to go with him, but the idea that he knew more about my past than I did was enough for me to take the risk. More importantly, I didn't know what or whom Beo had gone after and looking for him alone seemed just as risky.

I ducked into the car before I lost my nerve. Adric walked to the driver side door and slid in. Before I could blink, we were on our way.

"I cannot believe I just got into a car with Mr. Creepers. This is so surreal."

"Mr. Creepers? You called me dreamy."

"I said you have a dreamy smile. *Not* the same thing. A cabin in the woods? That's about as creepy as it gets." I turned to him. "Who is Beo after?"

"I'm not the only person hunting the ring. If I found it, someone else could. You could be in danger." Adric's voice had new tension. His emotions were a jumble of anticipation, excitement, and the blanket of calm covering what was really going on inside.

He drove ridiculously fast. Woods Landing was about a thirty-minute drive under normal circumstances. At this speed, we'd be there in fifteen minutes. I realized I was crushing the door handle in my grip. I released my hold and pressed my hands into my lap.

"The ring seems to allow me to read people's emotions and intentions. Does it work the same on everyone?" A rush of panic washed over me as I imagined people hunting the ring—and me.

"No. It doesn't work that way."

"That's incredibly vague." I turned my body to face his.

Adric took a breath and considered his words. "You went to a jeweler, and he couldn't tell you much about the ring, could he?"

I hesitated, and then nodded my agreement. "No one could tell me anything about it. I even sent it to Switzerland—dropped a small fortune and found out absolutely nothing."

"You sent it away?" His voice was accusatory.

"Last time I checked, the ring *is* mine. I was trying to learn more about it. And by the way, you haven't told me anything new."

His carefully guarded emotions cracked. Frustration peeked through stinging me with a hot vibration.

"It's extremely rare. The only one to ever exist."

My head spun. I blinked several times trying to focus. Was it the speed or the situation making me dizzy?

"You have no idea how your life is about to change." He rubbed the back of his neck.

For a moment, I could sense his emotional conflict—frustration and astonishment. Funny, that was exactly how I felt, with a hefty dose of terrified.

"I changed my mind. I'll sell you the ring…" I forced down a wave of nausea. "I just want to find Beo and go home." He didn't slow the car. "Pull over." Tempering my panic grew uncomfortable.

"We're almost there."

"I don't give a flying fuck where we *almost* are unless it's *almost to my truck*! Turn around, or I'm calling the police." I pulled out my phone.

Adric moved so fast I couldn't process what was happening. One second I was pushing buttons, and the next, he had my phone.

"Give it back!" I reached for the door handle. Jumping out was going to hurt.

"Wait! You don't understand." He pulled onto a dirt road, and in a matter of seconds, we were parking. "I'll try to explain things to you."

"Give me my phone. *Now.*"

Adric handed it over. "I want to figure this out too. The cabin—we're here. Come inside…please." He looked at me with pleading so obvious I didn't need the insight of his emotions to know there was something important he wanted to say.

I used what little focus I had left to reach out. It was becoming easier to identify what I was sensing. He was telling the truth.

"You have five minutes."

58

We both opened our doors and approached the cabin. I was shivering, but whether that was because of cold or nerves, I didn't know.

It was difficult to see the structure. I assumed it was similar to the others in this area of the Medicine Bow Range. I made out a small, log cabin surrounded by what appeared to be black holes—the absence of light where evergreen trees stood blocking what little illumination the moon provided. Adric unlocked the front door and switched on a light. I peeked inside.

The cabin had a lingering scent of mothballs. Inside, the décor was a combination of garage sale furniture and hand-me-down wall hangings. Nothing was imprinted. As a rental, that wasn't surprising. I decided to follow him in, but not before reaching into my pocket and grabbing the small four-inch switchblade knife I always carried. I concealed it in the palm of my hand.

Beyond the hodgepodge seating arrangement in the small living room was a U-shaped kitchen. The cabin continued to the right, where I guessed a bedroom and bathroom were located. I took a seat in the chair closest to the door.

"Start talking," I said.

He milled around the room, ignoring me.

"Damn it! I called you because you have answers. I broke all my own rules when I decided to meet with you. Somehow I've ended up here without my wolf in your creep-o-cabin. I don't know why I trusted you, but I did. Now, tell me what the hell is going on!"

My unbridled outrage snagged his attention. He sat on the couch and nodded, confirming some decision in his head. "The ring is a cultural relic. There's a small group of people trying to find it. It was made for someone like you, a Seer." He stopped and waited for me to process what he'd said.

"Someone like me?"

I'd spent years burying the hope of finding someone else like me. Being an orphan with no information about my history meant every person I met was a potential relative. If that wasn't enough, every person I met was also possibly seeing the world like I was. Eventually, I realized that went both ways.

I'd closed down that part of myself after discovering the disappointment that came with learning no one was like me, in any way. Adric had just ripped the doors off that particular part of my heart.

We both jumped at the sound of scratching.

"I told you he'd find us." Adric walked past me and opened the door.

Beo trotted inside. Front paws in my lap, he nuzzled and licked my face. I wrapped my arms around him and breathed in pine needles on damp fur.

"You stupid wolf. I should shoot you myself."

"You have a bad habit of character assassination." Adric closed the door and returned to the couch.

"What?" I asked the question with Beo still half in my lap.

"You called me creepy and now Beo is stupid. Neither of those statements is true. He tracked you down in less than half an hour. That's impressive, even for a companion wolf."

I was struck with an overpowering urge to close my eyes. Dizziness warped my vision, making me woozy and light-headed. I ran the earlier events of the night through my mind. There was no way Adric could've put anything in my drink. I hadn't had any lemonade after he arrived. The strange exhaustion that had been coming and going for months was back, and it was stronger.

I couldn't focus my eyes. The room spun. "Um…I…" My view narrowed to a tunnel of light haloed in a blur of color. "I don't feel…" Everything went black.

NINE

I woke in a strange bedroom and immediately took an inventory of myself—fully clothed, no injuries I could see, exhausted, but otherwise fine. Moving in slow motion to test my own stability, I cracked open the bedroom door. The salty aroma of frying bacon made my stomach growl. Beo sat outside the kitchen giving Adric his feed-me eyes.

Adric stood with his back against the kitchen counter. His wide shoulders and tall frame filled the small space. He wore a fitted, white tank and jeans. Muscles twitched in his arms as he opened a package.

He tossed a piece of raw bacon to Beo who snatched it in mid-air.

I opened the door and stepped into the abbreviated hallway.

"Good morning. How are you feeling?" Adric's nonchalant mood was enviable. I was a hot mess of nerves and confusion.

"What time is it?" I reached for my cell phone in my sweatshirt pocket—10:55 AM. Five missed calls from Jenny. "Shit!" I jogged out to the front porch and dialed.

"What the fu—."

"I'm sorry."

"Not taking my calls? Do we do that?"

"Jenny…I…" How was I going to tell her what happened? " I forgot to charge my phone." Instantaneous nausea roiled inside me. "I fell asleep. I wasn't ignoring your calls."

"What the hell. You were doing so well. Really trying move on, you know? But you've been so weird lately."

"I know. I'm just tired. I'm obsessed with this ring thing."

"At least you'll admit it." I heard children's voices in the background. "The bell is ringing. Damn it. I have to go. Call me later. Okay?"

"Yeah, I promise."

She ended the call.

"Food is ready." I jumped at the sound of Adric's voice. He stood inside the front door, making an obvious effort to give me space. "You must be hungry."

I shook my head, but my stomach growled loud enough for us both to hear.

"Eat something. You'll feel better."

I followed him to the table and sat. Adric placed a platter-sized plate in front of me—eggs, hash browns, bacon and toast. A steaming cup of coffee came next. The plate held enough food to feed three people, and I'd probably eat it all. Adric sat across from me with a cup of coffee.

"You aren't hungry?" I asked.

"I ate earlier."

"It's not poisoned, right?"

"You tell me." He shrugged in his annoyingly casual way.

"I don't care. I'm starving." My point was emphasized with another growl from my stomach. I picked up the fork and dug in. It was delicious. The warmth of the food made me feel human again. "I've never passed out before."

"Your breathing was normal, pupils were reactive." He half-shrugged. "You were sleeping. So I carried you into the bedroom and let you rest."

I didn't say anything. I wasn't sure if I should thank him or call the police.

"Do you want to continue our conversation from last night?" Adric asked.

I did want to know more—more about my sight, the ring, and my past. But I wouldn't be able to un-know whatever information he shared.

"Explain to me what you meant when you called me a *Seer*?" The word felt awkward in my mouth.

Adric nodded. "People tend to link race to skin color and ethnicity, but there's more to it. Race can also be a classification of specific characteristics. Your biological ancestry, in a way, can be your unique race." He paused. I maintained my silence. "You're a Seer. It's your biological heritage—your race, that gives you the ability to read and control emotional energy." He shifted in his seat. "It's a genetic mutation. Your brain works differently than the average human. Something in your genetic code has been…intensified." He took a long pause and glanced away before bringing his eyes back to mine. "Can I ask you a question?"

"I guess so."

"Tell me about your family."

My heart stopped. "I don't have much to tell."

"It's important." His upper body draped over the top of the table. Long, muscled arms rested inches from my plate.

I bit the inside of my cheek and leaned away. "I had amnesia as a child. I don't know anything about my biological family, not even where I came from before I showed up in Cattle Creek, Wyoming at the age of ten. My adoptive father raised me. He died about eight months ago."

"I'm sorry." I sensed a familiar emotion— numbness. He was well acquainted with loss.

"Are you a Seer?" I asked.

My chest tightened the longer the question hung in the air.

"No." The single word was a wrecking ball. I could feel my hope shatter in a million pieces. I silently prayed I could keep what was left of me from crumbling.

"Ione?" His brawny body took on a vulnerable quality as he slouched into his chair. Blue eyes found mine, and the depth and invitation in them lit something inside of me.

"I am like you," he said. "My parents are both dead—"

"The world is full of orphans. That doesn't make us alike." My words were empty. I hadn't meant to be cold, but I needed him to stop talking.

He continued anyway. "Have you ever heard of the Doctor's Trial?"

I hesitated. It seemed a strange direction to take our conversation. "Yes. I know about it, and the other eleven trials, the Trials of War Criminals before the Nuremberg Military Tribunals. They were trials for war crimes of German doctors who the United States authorities held after their occupation at the end of World War Two." His thick eyebrows rose. "I was a history major." I shrugged. "What does the trial have to do with anything?"

"Experiments were conducted on humans by the Nazi party."

Images flashed through my mind, black-and-white photographs I'd seen at the Holocaust Museum in Washington, D.C. on a high school history club trip. My insides twisted as I recalled the pictures of mutilated and tortured bodies discovered in the medical facilities located at various concentration camp sites throughout Nazi occupied Europe.

"The Nazis experimented with genetics. It was the dawn of the discovery of DNA, really." Adric shifted again, his legs straddled a table leg and his arms, once again, draped close to mine. "Through a process of breeding, they could intentionally recreate, improve, strengthen, or eliminate isolated genetic traits."

I shook my head. "I'm not sure I'm following."

"They had a particular interest in mind control." Adric waited for me to catch up.

"Maybe you don't understand what it is I see. I'm not psychic. I don't control minds." I narrowed my eyes.

He gave a half shrug. "Psychic abilities are vast. Your sight is certainly within the realm of what the Nazis were trying to perfect. The genetic traits they manipulated were varied. For whatever reason…" He shrugged again. "Your line of ancestry has some connection to emotional energy."

It made sense, sort of. The story was the closest thing to an explanation of my sight anyone had ever given me, but it was incredibly far-fetched.

"How do you fit into all this? Why do you know so much about Seers if you aren't one?"

Adric fiddled with his coffee cup. The liquid inside sloshed. He hadn't taken a single drink. "Because my race was a product of the same experiments. We call ourselves Vryzoldak. We're genetically enhanced like Seers, but our mutation is mostly physical. As I'm sure you know, the Nazis were obsessed with biological perfection." I nodded. "There was a purpose to the obsession beyond delusional belief of Arian superiority. An army of soldiers, who could withstand extreme environments, had exceptional strength and stamina, and unassailable immune systems would be unstoppable." He met my eyes. "And they could pass their genetic traits on to future generations of Nazi soldiers."

Adric stood and walked to the antique wood stove in the far corner of the living room. He reached behind it and gripped a cast iron poker used for moving logs in the fire.

I flinched.

"I'm not going to skewer you. I want to you touch this, make sure you know it's not a trick." He handed me the tool.

The rod was heavy cast iron and cold against my skin. "Okay?"

Adric held out his hand and I returned the poker. He bent the rod in half as if it was a pipe cleaner.

"What the…"

68

Adric turned to the fireplace and placed the bent rod on the hearth. "It's part of the Vryzoldak mutation—advanced strength."

"What you just did isn't advanced strength. It's impossible."

"And a psychic ability to see emotion, that's possible?" Adric stared me down from across the room. I could pick up on a slight indication of humiliation.

"Are you embarrassed?" A lukewarm emotion with low-level vibrations hit me next. He wanted me to feel safe. "You don't want me to be frightened."

Adric maintained his silence.

"How many Vry…" I stopped, trying to remember how he'd said it.

"Vryzoldak." He corrected.

"How many are there?"

"A million. Give or take a few." Adric settled into his chair.

"A million? A million people, mutants, or whatever…like you. I don't believe it."

He straightened in a way that made it impossible to ignore his size. "You can believe whatever you want. I'm telling the truth."

"Let's say you *are* telling the truth. There have been two, even three, generations since World War Two ended. How are there now one million of you? Wouldn't the genetics be, I don't know, diluted by now?"

69

"Vryzoldakianism is a dominant genetic mutation. It rides on DNA like a computer virus in the circuitry of a motherboard. It alters how genes are expressed. If you carry the mutation, your genes are affected." He shrugged like what he'd said was obvious.

I suddenly wished I'd paid more attention in freshman biology.

"What does the ring have to do with it?"

"The ring is kind of a," he paused, "Holy Grail. It's supposedly infused with Seer source energy." He looked at me to gauge my reaction.

For the first time in my life, I was on the other end of thinking someone in the room was crazy. I crossed my arms, holding them tight against my chest. "Go on."

"The best way to describe it would be to compare it to an endless source of electricity. Instead of producing electrical current, it amplifies a Seer's abilities. Honestly, before last night, I didn't understand why it was so important to find the ring. I was hired to find it and I knew there are others looking for it as well. I thought it was a game of ego for old, rich men." His eyes fixed on mine. "Then I met you."

"So?" I tilted my head.

"Ione…you're the last Seer." He stopped, watching me to see if I understood the gravity of what he'd said.

I didn't move a muscle. "What?"

70

"There's a group, the Crestere. They believe the genetic work of the Nazis was part of God's plan to return humans to their former perfection, a state of flawlessness that was lost after the fall from Eden. But, they also believe Seers are an abomination, that mind control and psychic powers are blasphemous."

His words rested heavy in my head. I pushed away my plate. The smell was suddenly making me sick. I thought better of wasting the food and placed it on the floor for Beo.

"The Crestere is a powerful organization. They've been active since before the war ended. The indoctrination of their belief system was part of the training they received as soldiers—"

"Soldiers?"

"The Crestere..." he paused. "It's entirely comprised of Vryzoldak."

"Like you?" My palms began to sweat.

Adric's face contorted "That's like saying all white men are members of the KKK."

"Are *you* a member of the Crestere?"

"No!" His face condensed into a wrinkled mask of disgust.

"But this group organized the murders of all the other people like me. And they'll kill *me* if they find me." A dense sensation of cold pressed against my skin. My head began to throb. "And the ring, they're after it too." Adric's jaw muscles twitched.

"I was told there are several collectors in search of the ring." He nodded. "It makes sense…if the Crestere had any reason to believe a Seer was alive, they'd want to keep the ring as far away from that person as possible,"

I started to take off the ring.

"Don't take it off. This might sounds strange…"

"For the love! What could possibly be more whacked-out than what you've already told me?" I snorted. "I think we're long past *strange*."

"It can't be tracked when you're wearing it. There are people with the ability to pick up on the ring's energy. There was some kind of protection against tracking it when it was hidden, but that protection is even stronger now that you're wearing it."

I spun the ring around my finger.

Adric's body pushed against the table as he closed the space between us. "When you found it in the chest, it became much easier for those of us tracking. The trail disappeared again when you started wearing it on your hand. It works that way because you're a Seer."

He ran his hand over his face. "I should've realized it the moment I saw it on your hand in the café. I couldn't sense it." He was talking to himself now.

A ripple of exhaustion shook my body. Panic followed. I couldn't pass out again. "Take me back to my truck. I'll give you the ring there. I'm not up for being a circus attraction." I sighed. "Or the target of some psychotic hate group."

A cold chill replaced my nauseated panic as I realized my safety teetered on Adric's willingness to keep my secret. "You won't tell anyone about me."

His eyes met mine. "No. I won't." He stood. "I'll take you back to your truck."

We didn't talk on the drive back to Laramie. Beo rode in the rear of the Mercedes and was comical in his discomfort. On the other hand, he seemed relaxed with Adric. I wasn't sure what changed, but Beo decided he was safe.

I wasn't as convinced. Adric's strength alone was an obvious threat, but more ominous was the information we'd shared. If he was telling me the truth, his knowing my secret was far more dangerous than I could ever have imagined. And he was Vryzoldak, just like every member of the Crestere.

The car stopped in the parking space across from my truck. We both stepped out. The closing doors made quiet echoes in the empty parking lot. I stepped to my truck and Adric blocked me. Leather and cloves filled my lungs. The physical proximity of his chest so close to mine made something in my throat catch.

"Call me if you have questions, or if you have any trouble." He tilted his head another inch closer to mine. "I don't want the ring just yet. Promise me you won't take it off." He was whispering.

73

"I don't want it." I shook my head. "If someone is close to finding it, and they find me—"

"Your chances of staying hidden are better with you wearing it because of how it affects your sight." He brought his face even closer. I could feel his breath. "It'll help you to know if someone is trying to hurt you."

His hands were suddenly at my sides. Warmth poured from his skin into mine. My body lit like tinder.

He cradled my face in his hands. His lips brushed my forehead. A wave of energy shot through me.

"Goodbye, Ione." Adric's breath caressed the moist skin where he'd kissed me. His scent filled my head. *God* he smelled good. I closed my eyes and took in another breath.

I opened my eyes. He was gone. The crushing sound of asphalt under tires told me his car was heading out of the lot. I reached up and touched my forehead. My skin was still wet from his kiss.

TEN

The TV was on in the background while I ate breakfast. I glanced at my watch—less than twenty minutes until my first shift in over a week. I'd told Jackson I had a sinus infection and needed time off. I'd told Jenny I had the worse case of PMS on record. I'd been telling *myself* I was overtired and needed rest. I was lying to everyone.

Adric had hijacked my brain and my body. I'd been exhausted for days after meeting him. I couldn't stop thinking about the hours we'd spent together.

I scooped another spoonful of oatmeal and tried to forget about Seers, Vryzoldaks, murders, and magic rings. I turned up the TV volume.

75

The morning news was the usual. The feature story covered a proposed smoking ban for the county. The local Shriner's chapter was gearing up for its annual fundraiser, and the weather forecast was typical for fall in Wyoming—cold and windy.

The anchor paused. "We're receiving breaking news. We'll be cutting to our national affiliate for the remainder of the program."

An aerial of a large one-story building filled the screen. *USOC Training Center, Colorado Springs, Colorado* appeared across the bottom of the picture.

The reporter's voice was breaking in and out. "We're told bodies were found inside the facility…unsure at this time of the method used to attack the athletes within the complex, but there are several reports…multiple dead and possibly more…"

The audio cut out. The screen changed over to show a talking head next to the aerial of the building. *Dr. Wayne Mullins*, labeled the man whose lips I could see moving but couldn't hear. I changed channels. All the stations were showing some visual form of the training center.

After watching the coverage and listening to the radio on the way into town, I learned as many as twenty training Olympians mysteriously died while in the U.S. Olympic Complex. There were no obvious injuries to the bodies and no indication of mass suicide. The whole situation was incredibly strange.

At the feed store, Jackson refused to speculate. He said it was a waste of time, and that the authorities would figure it out long before either of us. I was relieved to avoid the topic. Mass murder was something I was trying to erase from my mind.

I lost myself in the tedium of work tasks. The warehouse was behind on inventory since I'd taken time off. There was plenty of work to keep me busy. Hours raced by, and before I knew it, my shift was over.

I walked into the house and rummaged for something that might qualify as dinner. I flipped on the TV, and my appetite vanished.

Throughout the day, dozens of reports of single or multiple dead bodies were filed with various law enforcement offices. Each situation was eerily similar to the tragedy discovered at the Olympic Training Center. Among the dead were legendary athletes, political figureheads, doctors, lawyers, engineers, spiritual leaders, several mental health patients, college professors, and even an entire group of highly trained military armed forces specialists.

I filtered through the files in my head of tragedies I could remember from history. This was unlike any I remembered.

According to the reports, each of the groups or individuals killed were leaders in their fields, all highly-talented at one specific set of skills. All the victims were exceptional at something. I envisioned Adric and the cast iron fire poker.

My phone vibrated. I read the number and my heart stopped. "Adric?" Beo trotted past me and went to sit near the front door.

"I need to see you. Can I visit you at home?"

"Um…"

"It's important, Ione."

I watched images appear on the TV screen—bodies in black bags, panicked loved ones, and flashing emergency vehicle lights. "Okay. Where are you? I'll give you directions."

"I'm here." There was a knock.

I walked to the front of the house and opened the door. Adric stood outside.

I felt unsteady on my feet. "And you wonder why I nicknamed you Mr. Creepers? You knew where I live without me telling you. And you show up at my door while simultaneously asking if you can visit?" I stood in the doorway, blocking his way in. He looked just as good as the first, last, and every time I'd seen him.

At a solid six feet five inches, he made me feel small, which didn't happen often. He wore jeans, black boots, and his black, leather jacket. The dark gray color of his shirt made his eyes a darker blue than I remembered. His hair was the same, an appealing mess of blond haphazardly arranged on his head. His facial scruff was longer. An emotion I hadn't seen on his face before played across his features. He was guarding, but his exhaustion was palpable.

My comment solicited a lopsided grin, and Adric took on a relaxed stance and leaned into the doorframe. "Touché." He gave me a worn-out smile. "Can I come in?" His voice was rough like he'd been yelling…or crying.

I gestured for him to walk past me into the house. He headed for the couch. Beo followed. Adric turned to look at me. "You know why I'm here."

"The killings. The victims, they're people like us." I swallowed back nausea.

"Killings? So you've been able to see something." His shoulders sunk. A defeated and resigned heaviness took over his emotions.

I realized no one had reported the deaths as *killings*. "Uh…no. I don't actually *know* they were murdered."

Adric drilled me with icy, blue eyes. I sat down, closed my eyes, and tried to focus. The pressure of his depressed emotions in my head made me unstable. I felt Beo lie down on the floor beside me.

Behind closed eyes, the pictures I'd seen on the news—shots of various buildings and body bags— flashed through my mind. Like gears clicking into place, I felt something inside of me solidify. "They *were* murdered." I cupped my hand over my mouth. "How do I *know* that?"

"I don't know." He leaned back and ran his hands over his face. "Maybe because there are so many, there is some kind of emotional energy surrounding the victims you are able to pick up on with your sight." His eyes found mine. "It appears the victims are a variety of us. I've heard confirmed deaths of Vryzoldaks, Omnis, and Pharmaks, but the majority are Vryzoldak."

The pressure in my head doubled. "Wait. Who? What are Omnis and Pharmaks?"

Adric shook his head in agonized thought. "They are races. Similar to us, but with their own special set of mutations." He said it with exasperation.

He stared into the empty space of the room. "I need you to come with me. The Vryzoldak council is meeting tomorrow. You can help, and you'll be safe."

"What are you talking about?" My head continued to pound.

"I work for Alexander Odin. He's the Vryzoldak council leader. I can take you to him and put you in contact with all the members of the council. They can protect you, and if you can help them, maybe fewer will die if this insanity continues."

His voice was pleading. A growing energy of wild panic filled the room. It was abrasive against my skin, and grated on my nerves. Something was wrong. I looked into Adric's eyes. What hit me nearly took me to the ground. I gasped and clenched my fists. I was struck full-force with grief so heavy it threatened to take me under. "Oh, God. Make it stop."

"Ione?" He kneeled in front of me, resting his hands on my knees. I ached for comfort. My skin itched to be touched. There was a void where my chest had been.

"Who did you lose?" I was whispering, holding back tears

Adric closed his eyes. He reinforced his emotional block.

Relief. I could breathe.

He sat next to me. "My sister."

The short-lived moment of insight into his grief told me the loss was devastating. My body reached for him. His head dropped against my neck. My arms closed around his shoulders. The weight of his body as it melted into mine soothed the raw irritation his initial grief created. "I'm so very sorry."

His hands rested on the small of my back. The connection was electric, his fingers like conductors of emotional energy from one body to the next. Tingling in my spine warned me of a surge that was building between us. I released my arms.

Adric pulled away and sunk into the couch. "You aren't safe out here."

"No one knows about me except you." I created more space between us. Our energies ebbed the wider I made the distance. I needed the space to think clearly.

"That might not be true." His face turned to me.

"You said you weren't going to tell anyone." My throat was tight.

He sat up straight. "I didn't, but that day in Laramie at the restaurant? Beo ran after someone. We can't be sure it wasn't someone who knows what you are. Considering what happened today, I'd say you're lucky to be alive."

ELEVEN

I buckled into a car headed out of town three hours later. Beo and my duffel bag filled the back seat of the black Range Rover Adric was driving.

I'd spent two hours on my phone making arrangements. I talked George Niamith, the closest thing I had to a neighbor, into checking on the house. I called Jackson and made sure he could cover my shifts for the foreseeable future. Finally, I called Jenny.

Talking to Jenny about leaving Cattle Creek wasn't hard, but lying to her was excruciating. I told as much of the truth as possible without exposing the extent of how strange a turn my life had taken.

"I just have to get away for a while."

"Damn you, Ione! Why now? It's not safe. People are dying. This is scary. You're not yourself lately, and I'm worried."

"I'll be careful—I promise. It won't be for long. I just need some time, and I need you to trust me."

That was all it took—asking her to trust me. A few "okays" a couple of "love yous," and we hung up. My guilt was nauseating.

"Everything all right?" Adric asked.

I set my phone on my lap. Heartburn scorched in my chest. "I need you to fill me in on what the hell we're doing."

"I understand if you're anxious." Adric's voice wasn't overly patronizing, but I couldn't squelch the annoyance his comment evoked.

"I don't need to be coddled. I need to know what I've gotten myself into, just tell me the details."

"We're headed to Chicago where Vryzoldak headquarters are located. Alexander Odin, my boss, is the head of the council. He's called council to session because of what happened today." He took a deep breath. "Thanks for coming."

"Considering you believe I'm on some kind of hit list, and calling the cops to tell them some whack-job is killing all the super-humans isn't really an option, what choice did I have?" His grip tightened on the wheel. "What's the council?"

"The governing group for Vryzoldak. That doesn't matter. What's important is the fact that

Alexander has reason to believe the Crestere is behind the murders."

"Wait. They're killing their *own* people now?"

"They don't see it that way." He dropped one hand from the wheel and ran it through his hair. "They believe the council's decision to exist in secret—that's not the right word—to exist as *equals* to the rest of humanity, is weak. It's their belief that Vryzoldak are superior and should have power over the masses to make laws and use resources in a way that better benefits us specifically. It's an all-or-nothing mentality among Crestere members, and they've created a new generation more violent than any in the past."

"But why aren't they killing all the *inferior people*?" Even using the phrase for the purpose of my point made my skin crawl. Images of swastikas and striped black-and-white pajamas flashed through my mind.

"I'm not sure. That's one of the reasons I think you can help."

"Exactly how am I going to help?" The whole situation, on top of being a balance of horrifying and unbelievable, was confusing. I had so many questions.

He was quiet for several moments. "When we get to Chicago, you're going to say we just met. If Alexander or anyone on the council knows I found you and the ring, and failed to report either, it won't end well."

I hesitated. "*Report?*"

85

"You are the last Seer. And you're in possession of what is believed to be a powerful relic that's been missing for decades. Like I said—it wont' go over well."

I was quiet for a moment. "Do you honestly think they'll believe we just met, and I decided to go half way across the country with you?"

"It wouldn't be the first time I persuaded a woman to go somewhere with me." He raised his brows as he said it.

"Right." I couldn't disguise the annoyance in my voice. Of course, he probably had a harem of women following him everywhere he went. "Well, for the record, I'm not the type—"

"There's something else I want to tell you."

"That's usually an intro into bad news." I picked up my phone and began to rotate it in my hands. It slipped through my fingers and dropped to the floor.

"I was in Laramie chasing the trail of the ring and ended up in a bar." He shifted in his seat. "You were there…and there was a man."

I froze mid-way to reaching for my phone on the floorboard. "That was you at The Big Horn. The asshole—I mean, you were the one who took that asshole out back after Jenny and I left the bar. We saw you in the alley when we drove off."

I sat up and looked at Adric. He nodded. "What did you do to him?"

86

"Nothing he didn't deserve." He gripped the wheel with both hands.

"You didn't, like…kill him, did you?" My heart raced. I didn't believe he would kill anyone, but then again, I didn't really know anything about him.

"No! I didn't kill him." He answered irritated.

"Why didn't you tell me before?"

He shrugged. "It was a coincidence."

Pinpricks stabbed at in the bottom of my stomach. Familiar nausea began to bubble. Something was *off.* "You're lying."

Adric whipped his head around. We made eye contact then he immediately fixed his eyes on the road. Silence filled the car.

"I'm not used to being called a liar." His voice was tight and teetered on giving away the anger he held at bay. "I'm also not used to someone being able to read my mind."

"It doesn't take a mind-reader to sniff out a liar." His accusation stung. I hadn't meant to violate his privacy. "Your emotions gave away your lie." I sighed in attempt to lighten the heaviness settling into my body. "I didn't mean to pry or make my way into someplace I wasn't invited."

I peered out my window at the side-view mirror. The last lingering beams of sunlight shot through billowing thunderheads in coral threads as the sun dipped below the horizon behind us.

Adric understood more about me than anyone I'd met, but he still didn't fully understand.

"It's like the sun." I felt him shift in his seat directing more of his attention to me. "The energy I see, it's kind of like sunlight. It's hard to bock out. It changes all the time, and even when I close my eyes, I can still feel it." I kept my eyes on the horizon.

"I didn't know I was lying." His anger was gone. "I thought it was just a coincidence. Now, I'm not so sure. There's something…I don't know, energy, maybe similar to what you described. It was leading me to you before I knew *you* were what I was after."

"You mean the ring's energy was leading you. I had it that night, on a chain around my neck."

He kept his eyes focused on the road. Mild tension filled the car. Heat rushed through my body.

"No. The ring is different." The intensity of his voice thundered through me. "I'm going to drive straight through. We should be there in twelve hours as long as we keep making good time. You should sleep. I'll wake you when I stop for gas."

"We can take turns driving."

"I'll be fine. The council is meeting mid-morning. This drive has to be as quick as possible. You should rest."

He was already driving well beyond the speed limit. Knowing he was racing against the clock made me nervous. Closing my eyes and checking out was inviting.

"I'll try to sleep but just for little while. Wake me when we stop."

He nodded.

I had at least twelve hours to drill him. A short snooze wouldn't hurt, and it wasn't much of a choice anyway. Nowadays, when sleep wanted to take me, it did. I cuddled down into my coat and drifted off.

TWELVE

We were somewhere in Eastern Nebraska when Adric woke me. I wiped the sleep from my eyes and shuffled into the convenience store. The florescent lights were too bright for my tired eyes but not bright enough to see everything in the store adequately. I used the bathroom, found snacks for myself, and grabbed a couple of packets of lunchmeat for Beo.

The woman at the counter was haggard and missing more than a few teeth. Those that remained were stained from cigarette smoke, which lingered in the air. Her hair was a stringy mess that lay lifeless around her face. She wore a blue, button-up shirt with the station logo and a pair of loose fitting jeans.

My stomach turned over when I noticed her wedding ring—a thin, plain, gold band with the purple imprint of fear. My eyes met hers, and I was slammed with a vision from her past.

A younger version of the woman changed clothes in front of a full-length bedroom mirror. Her slight frame and thin hair were familiar. The face smiling in the mirror showcased full pink lips and rich brown eyes. An even row of white teeth highlighted a petite face. She beamed freshness and youth.

A red, satin dress cascaded down her shoulders as she dropped it over her head. She checked herself in the mirror. As she turned to head out of the bedroom, a man twice her size stomped through the door. The weight of his steps created tiny earthquakes forewarning of a greater future destruction.

"What the hell?" He raked his gaze down her body. "I didn't marry a whore!"

An open fist stuck her face. The mirror wobbled, blurring her reflection as her body made contact with the hardwood. A sharp flash shot through my own body as she cried out. I felt her cutting shame as she touched the red welt growing across her cheek.

I blinked several times and realized I was standing frozen in the convenience store. I'd whelped out loud as I'd watched the ghost of her past take the beating.

"That all you want?" She spoke words void of emotion. What I'd seen was long in the past. She stood before me now completely numb. I paid and hurried out the door.

"Adric?" I looked around the parking lot. It was empty. He must've been in the bathroom.

The filling station was a solitary sign of civilization among endless cornfields. I took Beo for a walk behind the store. Light from streetlamps made the gas station exterior blindingly bright and flooded the surrounding open fields. Unfortunately, the lights did nothing to diminish the cold. I stood shivering in the dark, trying to keep an eye on Beo as he wove in and out of endless rows of dead cornstalks.

I walked back to the car and stopped just within the edge of the field to watch Adric. He tucked his phone into the front pocket of his jeans and rested against the vehicle. His powerful body was relaxed. Wearing only his gray T-shirt and jeans, his arms, hands, and face were all exposed to the bitter nighttime air. If I hadn't been standing outside fighting to keep from solidifying into an ice cube, I'd have thought it was a mid-July night. I took the last few steps into the parking area.

"You ready?" He hadn't turned to face me.

"Do you have eyes in the back of your head? And aren't you cold?"

Adric turned around. "You reek of bologna. I could smell you coming. And, no. It's a Vryzoldak thing."

The flush of embarrassment crawling up my face burned my freezing cheeks. "Right." I wiped my hands on my jeans. "I'll, uh, be right back."

"No. We need to go. Here." He handed me a damp paper towel used to clean the windshield.

The blue liquid on the towel was glacial. Rubbing the cloth over my numb hands made my skin raw. I hissed.

"Damn. You're half frozen." Adric took the paper towel and tossed it into the garbage. "Get in the car." He held my hand and pulled me to the passenger side door. The contact created a dull ache.

I pulled away.

Adric turned to me. "What?"

"What's wrong with me?"

"What do you mean? What's going on?"

My body was convulsing with shivers. It wasn't just the cold. It was the energy from the memory of the woman in the store and whatever Adric had transferred into my body when we touched.

"In the store, when I paid for my stuff. The woman at the counter—I saw a memory from her past. It was awful. That's never happened. And just now, when you touched me...what's going on with you? Your emotions are ...painful."

Adric said nothing. A wrinkle of confusion creased his forehead. I rested my hand over his heart where it thundered under his shirt. The dull ache I'd felt when his hand touched mine grew into a tsunami of emotional energy.

93

I saw a woman. She looked like Adric—blond hair, striking blue eyes, the same serious set to her jaw. She *felt* like him too.

"Your sister." Realization dawned. I shuddered at the depth of his grief.

Adric closed his eyes and stepped back. The confusion pasted across his face morphed into visible anguish. Just my mentioning her caused pain. When his eyes opened a moment later, despair met me and carved a hole in my chest.

"We need to go."

I let my hand fall and reached for the car door. "I'm sorry. I didn't mean—"

"Just get in."

The silence inside the car was suffocating. I sat staring at my hands waiting for him to speak, start driving, or…do something.

"She was a lot like you." He said it under his breath, but his words were clear enough in the quiet. His voice was stronger when he continued. "Naomi and I were inseparable most of our lives. About four years ago, we had an argument that changed everything. She didn't agree with my decision to go work for Alexander. I'm a tracker. It's what I do. She understood, but she didn't like me doing it for him. She despised the idea of me entering into any kind of political circle." He paused again. "She was brilliant, independent—to the point of being a real pain in the ass, and she was beautiful. She's been living in Cambridge the past couple of years. She was the youngest chemistry professor on staff at MIT." His pride felt velvety. "She was killed this morning on campus in her office." His emotional energy changed, turning once again into hollow aching. "Our mother died when we were children, and our dad when we were eighteen."

"You're twins?"

He nodded. "We need to go." He started the car. The noise of the engine closed a door on our conversation.

We barreled down the interstate. Next to the road, endless crop fields filled the landscape before being swallowed in a sea of blackness. They rose and fell according to the subtleties of the rolling hills. Moonlight highlighted cornstalks and was lost in the valleys between rows. The quick altering of dark to light made me dizzy. I turned to Adric.

He'd relaxed since we'd left the gas station. He drove with one hand loosely gripping the steering wheel. His giant hands made the wheel look like a toy. His other hand absently skimmed back and forth across his lips. In the dark of the car, I could see only the shadows and outlines of his body. The lights of the dash highlighted his cheekbones and thick eyelashes.

He glanced at me. "After our mother died, my father became depressed. Naomi reminded him so much of our mother—even her voice was the same. My father...his cure for everything was alcohol. As far as he was concerned, sober enough to know only your own name was sober enough."

"I'm sorry." My voice was small in what was suddenly the vast space of the car's interior.

"Naomi dropped out of school to babysit him—keep him from hurting himself and others. A Vryzoldak on a bender is pure disaster potential. After he died, she learned everything she'd missed, got a GED, and was enrolled in her undergraduate work in less time than it took me to finish high school." Adric leaned his head against the headrest. "My father finally drinking himself to death was the best thing he ever did for us."

"What about her funeral, shouldn't you be…"

"She was married. Her husband is taking care of it. Like I said, things between us the last few years…we weren't close anymore." He grew quiet.

"Was she happy? I mean, was she able to do the things she'd wanted, after your father died?"

"I think so. She was meant for her work in chemistry. I think she was happy in her marriage."

"Well, that's worth something; knowing the person you loved was happy, even if only for a short time."

The strange tension in the car evaporated.

"I suppose it is."

He'd made a conscious choice to share intimate parts of his life with me. A radiating heat swelled in my chest, pushing me to share some of myself with him.

"Do you really believe I'm the last Seer?" I asked.

He looked at me with intrigue. "I don't know." He framed it as a question. "Were you hoping to find your family?"

"I have so many questions about myself. It's all so strange. *I'm* so strange." I paused. "It's lonely trying to figure it all out." I rested my head against the headrest. "I'd like to know where I come from." I closed my eyes. "But Beo, Jenny, and my dad are my family. Finding out about my history won't change that." I fixed my eyes on the road ahead.

Adric didn't say anything. The quiet moments between us weren't uncomfortable, but there was heaviness to them. A groggy sensation built in my head, and dizziness washed over me.

"Do you know why I'm so tired all the time? It's like I just shut down—like I don't get to choose anymore when I'm awake and when I'm asleep. It's got to have something to do with my sight." I yawned out the last sentence.

He thought for a moment. "Your body has to balance all the emotions you're taking in. You must be having a problem with the increase in intensity the ring creates. When we get to Alexander's, there'll be council members who know more about Seers, how your mutation affects your body and brain. Is it a problem?"

"When isn't narcolepsy a problem?" I rubbed my eyes.

Adric laughed.

"Who's on the council? Would I know any of them? Are there famous Vryzoldak?" I yawned again.

Adric answered, but sleep took me before I made sense of his words.

THIRTEEN

The Vryzoldak council didn't meet in a conventional building. They were convening at a private estate in the Chicago suburbs. A *Welcome to Kenilworth* sign announced the area as we drove into an affluent neighborhood.

We parked in a circular drive tucked in a grove of maple trees and walked to a breathtaking colonial-style mansion. The sun peeked over the eastern horizon washing the white Masonite siding in a bath of gold. The home and extensively manicured grounds must have been worth millions. There were security personnel everywhere. It was more like the

White House than a private home in Illinois. I immediately felt out of place.

Adric informed me the council met here, but the house was also Alexander Odin's home. One of a number of properties he owned around the world.

Beo was a major disruption to the activities at the mansion. Security didn't give me a second glace until they noticed the giant wolf trailing us. Once they realized what he was, there was a lot of hushed talking on radios and nodding back and forth between men in dark glasses. I couldn't help myself and rolled my eyes more than once.

All the guards were easy to read. None of the security detail had an emotional wall like Adric. I wasn't sure if they couldn't block their emotions or they chose not to.

I was searched at our third security checkpoint. Bruiser, the security guy—quite possibly his real name, wasn't at all concerned about being discrete. His giant paws groped and mauled me.

"Hey!" I yelped as he stuck a hand down my right front pant pocket. Beo growled and moved closer to the man. Bruiser took his hand out of my pocket with impossible speed.

"Well, what's this?" He held my pocketknife.

I could feel the clamminess of his emotions—a sexed-up power trip. It was revolting. Beo took another step closing the gap between himself and the oaf holding my knife.

"No weapons allowed inside." Bruiser put it in his own pant pocket.

"Give me my knife, or I'll have my wolf retrieve it. My guess is he won't be gentle on the other small things in those pants." I straightened my shirt and jacket where Bruiser had mangled my clothing.

I looked up to watch Adric step between Beo and the man. "I think he want's you to return the woman's item." His eyes landed on Beo, whose snarls were growing louder. There was a smirk on his face that revealed he outranked the security troll.

"I told the girl, no weapons allowed inside. Now, call off the mutt." Bruiser's energy was quickly changing to a vibrato of electric anxiety.

Adric said nothing and stepped back to allow Beo another six inches closer to the other man. Bruiser reached into his pocket and tossed the knife into the air. I stepped forward to catch it. He turned to face Adric.

"Liability of the tart is on you, Tracker." Bruiser turned and walked to a group of security members who had come to watch the scene.

Beo and I followed Adric into the house.

"Can you really see what's in his pants?" Adric asked with a grin, as he opened the door from the vestibule into the foyer.

"You'll never know." I walked past him with Beo trailing behind me.

The interior was a strange combination of modern conveniences wrapped in antique packaging. The carpets and window treatments were done with heavy fabrics in shades of velvety reds. I caught a quick glimpse of a small table imprinted with a medium-tone blue hue.

Blue imprints were the most dynamic. The intensity of each color expressed the depth of the sadness imprinted. Sadness itself was dynamic—an emotion connected to many others. The table was shrouded in muted azure—sadness tinted with grief.

I expected more imprints in a house furnished with antiques. There were none as far as I could see.

We sat and awaited Alexander's arrival in what I assumed was his office. I balanced myself on the edge of an oversized wingback chair. I tensed as Beo and Adric stood. A gentleman about my height stepped into view.

"Hello." The man had a faint accent I couldn't place. "And who might this be, Adric?" His voice was slow and even, as if he calculated every syllable.

He nodded to Adric and smiled at me. It didn't provoke a smile in return. His short, fair hair was styled forward toward his face. The black tint of his eyes was emphasized by pale skin. I placed him in his late fifties. His stature was average, but with an unmistakable air of power.

The man had something tucked into a pocket of his vest under his suit jacket. It had the same maroon imprint as the ring. I stopped myself from gasping aloud.

"Alexander, this is Ione McCreery. Ione, this is Alexander Odin, High Minister of the Vryzoldak Council." Adric's voice was crisp and professional, a far cry from the casual calmness I'd become used to in our conversations.

"How nice to make your acquaintance, Ms. McCreery. I extend to you my welcome and offer you my humble accommodations. *Heil ok sæl.*"

I didn't understand whatever he'd said at the end of his greeting. The language was something I'd never heard. '*Heil*' made me uncomfortable even if it wasn't what it sounded like. Alexander's emotions were inaccessible. If I thought Adric was guarded, Alexander was Fort Knox. I'd barely tap into his intentions before draining myself of my own energy. I wasn't about to try.

"You are stunning, my dear." He bowed, took my hand and kissed it. The contact was clammy, his lips cool and sticky-wet. I gritted my teeth.

"Nice to meet you, Sir." Alexander made my insides squirm. Fighting the urge to move away from him was difficult. I took back my hand.

"Please, call me Alexander. Who is this?" He raised his brows.

"His name is Beo. I'm sorry if he caused problems with your security." I ran my fingers through Beo's neck scruff.

"Ah, the mighty Beowulf. How appropriate. I'm sure keeping him out would have created far greater problems." Alexander gave me a sly grin. "A companion wolf, how fascinating. And she wears the ring. Adric…how long have you been keeping this treasure from me?"

Adric appeared far more comfortable than his emotions revealed. A throbbing energy of apprehension pressed against my skin.

"Minister, I tracked the ring to Ms. McCreery and realized after meeting her that she's a Seer." Something in the room changed as he said it. Alexander's emotions momentarily opened. The effect was nauseating. I was relieved when he blocked them again. "We came to Chicago right away. In fact, we just arrived. Knowing the council was meeting, and under the circumstances, it seemed best to bring her here."

"And from where exactly did you come?"

"Wyoming." I said it before Adric could say anything more specific, and hoped Alexander would move on to other subjects.

He stared at me like he was trying to memorize my face. I focused on Beo to cut the intensity of his gaze.

"Wyoming is quite beautiful, if I recall correctly. I think it a strange place to find the *only* surviving Seer." He gave me another of his terrifying grins.

There was a knock at the door. Alexander peeled his eyes off me and looked to the door. "It's time. Please, follow me."

Adric, Beo and I shadowed Alexander through a series of rooms to a small elevator. We descended as soon as the doors closed. When they opened, we entered a large room set up for the meeting.

I realized with a rush of nerves that I was surrounded by Vryzoldak. They were normal people, if looking like professional athletes was normal. One of the men I recognized. He'd won several gold medals in the most recent Summer Olympics. I racked my brain, trying to remember his name. The media christened him *Ironman* because he'd received a heart transplant as a child and went on to become one of the world's fastest sprinters.

The Nazi party may have been advocating for an Aryan Nation, but the Vryzoldak in the room were not in any way a reflection of that belief. A mixture of men and women stood about the room, varying in height, weight, and coloring. All were relatively attractive people and obviously of superb physical fitness despite a significant range in age. Emotionally, they were all easy to read. I caught feelings of agitation, anger, curiosity, and even boredom.

One woman caught my attention. She wore a coral-colored sari embellished with gold stitching in a pattern of lotus flowers. Her long black hair framed her flawless amber skin. She smiled, and welcoming energy engulfed me.

The congregation approached their seats. Alexander left us standing in the center of the room. He sat in the middle of a large table with the other council members flanking him on both sides.

"Council, I present to you Ione McCreery. It appears our tracker has discovered the last Seer." The room inhaled in unison. "She also wears the Ring of Mar'eh."

Again there was an audible gasp. I self-consciously hid my ring finger under my thumb and placed my hands behind my back. The council clapped, and one-by-one they stood in ovation.

The emotion in the room intensified. I could sense hope, relief, greed, desire, anxiety, jealousy, and…fear. It was difficult to take in. Beo growled, and I reached for him. Adric put a hand around my waist.

The room spun. I closed my eyes, pleading with myself to calm down. It wasn't working, and the intensity built. Emotions stacked on top of one another, forming a suffocating weight on my chest.

I opened my eyes and was locked in a gaze with Alexander's soulless eyes. He opened the gates holding back his emotions, and they flooded my mind in a raging cloud of black.

FOURTEEN

"Shhhh, child. You're safe. Calm down." A hand stroked my head.

The woman I'd noticed earlier was even more beautiful up close. Dark, charcoal liner outlined hazel eyes. A small red bindi dot rested in the center of her forehead.

"Where am I? What happened?"

I tried to sit upright. Sore muscles protested. I placed my palm on my pounding head and closed my eyes.

"Careful, pet. You suffered a seizure. You've been sleeping for several hours. Your companion and

I have been taking care of you." She smiled and nodded toward the end of the bed.

"Beo, good boy," I whispered. He jumped onto the bed and lay beside me.

"He's beautiful. It's been so long since I've seen a companion. It warms my heart to watch the two of you."

I was taken back by the emotions pouring out of her, a warm, deep-seeded love tangled with longing.

"Who are you?" I shook my head. "I'm sorry. I should thank you for taking care of me. I don't know what happened. I've never had a seizure before."

"My name is Kali Gupta. I'm a member of the council. I'm happy to help." She rested her hand on mine. Heat pulsed through the contact and relaxed my aching body.

I slid my hand out from under hers. "Ms. Gupta, where's Adric?"

"Please, call me Kali. I was tired of his hovering, so I found work for him." She smiled again.

"Did anyone feed Beo?"

"We did try, but he refused to eat. That's normal for a companion. Why don't I get you both something?" She stood and walked toward the door. "I'll be back in a moment. Please, wait for me before you try to walk. You may need help." She smiled one last time and left the room.

I clumsily propped myself up with a pillow and leaned against the headboard.

Kali returned, and Beo and I both ate. She helped me stand. When she was sure I was capable, she left so I could shower.

I unzipped my duffel bag. Sitting on top of my clothes was a small note written on thick stationary.

Ask for me.
-Adric

I thought about peeking out the door to find him, but he would walk into the room in all his underwear-model glory, and there I would stand—awkward with epic bedhead.

I limped to the bathroom. It was spacious and beautiful, like the rest of the house, but more modern than the décor in the main foyer or Alexander's office. The scorching water rushing out of the oversized showerhead was a welcome sensation.

I reluctantly turned off the water and stepped out of the shower. In the half-fogged mirror, I studied by body. I anticipated bruises from top to bottom. Outwardly, I appeared the same. My hair hung damp over my shoulders. My long torso and longer limbs were the same body parts I'd lived in pre-seizure.

I dressed slowly, opting for jeans, a fitted, white tee, and short, brown, leather dress boots. I preferred my work boots, but horse manure in Alexander's multi-million-dollar mansion didn't seem appropriate. Thinking of Alexander sent a chill through me.

Beo paced at the bedroom door and whined.

"How long have you been inside, buddy?" I patted his head. "Okay, let's see if we can find the backyard."

Once outside, I realized calling the manicured lawns a backyard was absurd. The house sat on several densely wooded acres with the majority of the trees clustered along the perimeter. Multiple beds of various shrubs and ornamental grasses decorated the remaining open spaces. The sun kept me warm while I waited.

I tilted my face to the sky and closed my eyes. Standing outside in the quiet with just the wind and the sun transported me home. Maybe if I stood still long enough, when I opened my eyes I'd find myself standing in the back pasture a few hundred feet from the house.

"I've been looking for you." I startled. "Sorry. I didn't mean to scare you."

I turned to see Adric pushing his hands into his pockets. There were moments when he acted more like a nervous teenage boy than the giant superhero-like man he was. The muscles in his arms twitched in flexion as he pushed his hands deeper. I could feel his relief at seeing I'd recovered.

I smiled. "It's okay." His smile back was intoxicating. "I saw your note. I didn't want to interrupt your work."

"You wouldn't have interrupted." Adric took a step closer.

When he was near enough for me to whisper, I asked, "What happened?"

"I'm not sure." He shook his head.

"It was like I couldn't handle all the emotions at once. I tried to push it all back, but Alexander, he sort of opened up. That's when I...seized, or whatever."

It was Alexander that put me over the edge. That much I knew. There was something different about him. He wasn't like anyone else in that room. I couldn't tell what exactly was different.

"Tell me more about Alexander," I asked, hoping Adric might know what I didn't.

"He's the High Minister of the council—the leader of the Vryzoldak." I nodded. "He's a good leader. He's effectively kept peace among our people, and until now, he's kept the Crestere under control."

I hesitated, unsure of how to talk to Adric about what I sensed from Alexander.

"What?" He asked, guessing at my apprehension.

"It's just, he feels..." I whispered, "...dangerous."

"You sound like my sister," he huffed. "His responsibilities are endless, and his job isn't easy. Maybe you should keep that in mind."

Anger bubbled. "*Maybe* Naomi was right." Neither of us spoke for several moments. "Why is it you and he are guarded, and the others, like Kali, aren't?"

Adric shrugged. "We're both trackers. Not all Vryzoldak are trained. Trackers are taught to block emotions to keep decision making based in reason."

"I guess that explains why everyone else here is so easy to read."

"I wouldn't tell them that." Adric smirked.

"Alexander is a tracker?" I thought about it for a moment. "He had something in his vest pocket, a watch or some kind of jewelry. Do you know anything about it?"

"His pocket watch?" He nodded. "It was a gift from his wife. He wears it all the time. Why?"

I scanned the yard to be sure we were still alone. "It's imprinted…" I trusted Adric, but I didn't trust Alexander, and that complicated things. "Just made me curious." I shuffled my feet. "So, what's the plan now? I assume the council made decisions while I was…sleeping."

"They suspect the Crestere, but without the group taking credit, pursuing them can't be sanctioned by the council. They've decided to send a team to track down the Crestere leader, Cyrus Reid, to collect evidence. If the team can provide enough proof to secure unilateral approval, the council can take action." Adric's nervous energy sailed on tiny vibrations in the air. I caught a whiff of cloves as he stepped closer.

"What kind of action?"

"Whatever is necessary to end the attacks."

My throat constricted with the idea of what that might entail. "And by team, you mean…"

"Your ability to read Cyrus will serve as part of our evidence. Kali and Simon Brown have volunteered. Between the four of us, we have a tracker, technical support, an accomplished and respected diplomat, and a Seer. If *we* can't figure out how they're doing it, we've no chance of finding out how to stop them." Adric reached out and grabbed my hand. "It isn't going to be easy. If it were possible, I'd do it without you. This isn't what I envisioned when I brought you to meet Alexander. With the council in agreement, it isn't something you can refuse." His remorse was thick. It made my chest tight.

"What if I pass out again, or have another seizure? How do they even know I'm a Seer? There's no guarantee I can help, or that I'll be able to *see* anything." I pulled my hand out of his grasp.

"You're a Seer whether you want to be or not. There's no mistake about it, and you'll be ready by the time we leave." Professional Tracker Adric was back. "We hope to intercept Cyrus before the Crestere attack again, but we don't have much time. You'll need to start training."

"What kind of training?" A bolt of anxiety charged through me.

"I've been doing some research, talking with the other council members. There's a way to control your sight. I was right. It's the energy that's making you exhausted to the point of passing out." He paused. "Energy is what makes up everything, especially emotion. When you read someone, you're physically taking in emotion. Like any energy, there's a system for safely dealing with it. We'll help you learn how to handle it, so it doesn't overwhelm you."

I couldn't imagine telling Alexander no. Running away from a council of mutant superheroes was laughable.

"It will only help you. You'll learn how to control your sight. You're safe here with me. We can figure this out."

"God, I hope you're right."

FIFTEEN

My "Last Seer" status made me a celebrity among the council members and their families—most were staying at the mansion until they knew if it was safe to return home. The seemingly ever-expansive shelter of Alexander Odin's protection would have been impressive if he wasn't so damn scary. I avoided him as much as possible. The one council member I was always happy to see was Niko Berkovitz.

Niko was the oldest member of the council. He spent countless hours with Adric and me. A truly kind man, his emotional energy was steady, never too much of anything. His extensive knowledge and experience made him the perfect council member to

115

serve as Official Historian. Niko was a WWII survivor, born and raised for the first five years of his life in one of the medical facilities under Nazi control. He was a first-generation Vryzoldak.

"Ironically, it wasn't until about nineteen fifty-five, with the help of resistance to the Civil Rights Movement, that the Crestere gained support for their initiative against Seers."

Niko's voice was melodic, his French accent lightly touching only certain words. "Albert Reid, Cyrus's father, was adamant Seers were dangerous. He was devastatingly effective with his rhetoric—skilled at playing on fear. In a few short decades, he managed to orchestrate genocide of the entire race." Niko shook his head. "When Cyrus took over the organization after his father's death, things changed again. Cyrus's hatred is pervasive. No one is immune. Vryzoldak or otherwise, if you do not agree with his doctrine, you are to be eliminated."

Niko remained steady and calm. But in his watery gray eyes was a reflective quality only possible when someone spoke of events they'd witnessed.

"How am I here? I mean…if Seers have been hunted since the fifties, where did I come from?

Niko took a deep breath. "That, my dear, I do not know." He lifted his narrow shoulders. "Someone didn't want you to be found, and they did an exceptionally fine job of hiding you."

"Do you think it's possible my parents might still be alive?"

He patted my hand and closed his weary eyes. "I'm sorry." He shook his head with a heaviness that didn't require further answer.

Pain welled in my chest. "Will you try to find information in your genealogical files? Anything, no matter how small, might help me find some answers. I came from somewhere."

His face tripled in wrinkles as he smiled. "We all come from somewhere, dear. Sometimes it's better to focus on where we're going instead of where we've been." Niko patted my hand once more before he stood. "I'll see what I can find." He returned to his work.

My phone buzzed in my pocket.

"It's Jenny," I said to Adric. "Hello?"

"Hey, girl. You still in Chicago?"

"Yeah. It's not so bad—I've met some pretty great people." I flashed a grin at Adric. Kali walked into the room and sat with us.

"Actually, one of them just walked in the room." I pressed the speaker button. "Say hi, Jenny."

"Hi Jenny." Jenny repeated.

"Okay, smart ass—say hi to Kali."

Kali leaned toward the phone. "Hi Jenny. Nice to meet you. I've heard so much about you. Ione misses you even more than her beloved Wyoming, I'd venture."

"Oh yeah? Maybe she should come back then—see us both. I imagine the youth hostel situation is getting pretty old. Ione, you sick of pooping for an audience yet?"

Adric laughed. I narrowed my eyes at him.

"You didn't introduce Manly-Man," Jenny said.

"That's because I was only introducing you to the *great* people I've met."

"Umhum—but not the sexy ones," she replied. "Hey—take me off speaker."

I put the phone to my ear. "What? What's going on?"

"Somebody broke into your house last night. There doesn't seem to be any major damage. They made a mess—dug through drawers, but as far as I can tell, nothing is missing. I'm waiting on the Sheriff to get here."

"Leave it, Jenny. You shouldn't be there."

"Calm down. I'm not here alone. Old man Niamith called me. He came to check on the house this morning and found the mess. It looks like some high school kids found out it was empty and decided to have some fun—destructive fun."

"Jenny…" I couldn't form the words I wanted to say. How was I going to tell her there were people looking for a magic ring and the last living Seer? How was I going to tell her that person was me?

"Yeah?"

"Don't worry about the mess. Just ask George to change the locks, and let me know what I owe him. Stay away from the ranch. There's nothing valuable there. If it wasn't bored kids and someone dangerous broke in ...it's better if no one is there."

I heard her sigh. "So you're not coming back."

"Not yet."

She cleared her throat. "Let me talk to Manly-Man."

"What? No! Why?"

"Manly-Man! I need to talk to you!" She shouted loud enough for the entire room to hear.

Adric held out his hand. "I'm being paged?" I placed the phone in his palm. "Yes?"

Adric's eyes met mine. The muscles in his jaw flexed. He remained silent. I could hear Jenny's voice in clips. Adric nodded and drummed the table top with his free hand.

"I see," he said. His weight shifted in his chair. "I understand. I will tell her." He ended the call.

"What the hell?" I stared at him. "Tell me what?"

"Not you." He turned to Kali, "Jenny wanted me to tell you it was nice meeting you."

"What?" I drilled a glare into the phone.

"Jenny said to call her next when you're on your way home. She also said you need to call the old man yourself and that if I'm the same psycho who visited you at the feed store, you're incredibly stupid."

"Damn her." I stood.

"That's not all. She said she misses you, and she loves you. She just can't deal with your stubborn ass right now." He smirked.

"Unbelievable."

"I like her," Kali added with a smile.

"I don't." I huffed.

"Ione—someone broke into your house?" Adric wasn't smiling any more.

"Dumb kids getting off on some lightweight vandalism." I shrugged.

"We should discuss it with Alexander." He stood to go. "Kali, will you touch base with Simon. We may need to look into this a little more." Adric's body language changed. He was in Tracker mode. "Ione, I'll find you for some training in about an hour. I'm sure Niko will stay with you until then."

"Are you going to pay him the normal babysitting rate?"

Adric halted at the door. "Alright then. Training session starts now."

"Fantastic." I deadpanned and followed Adric to a vacant room on the second floor of the mansion.

While I was grateful for the council's willingness to help me manage my sight, I was not eager for their help after I had a few sessions under my belt. I spent five days with a number of different council members all purposely trying to force me into a coma.

Sessions consisted of twenty to thirty minute trainings where I was subjected to every imaginable emotion. There were moments of joy and laughter, but the heartbreaking memories consisting of tragic flashbacks and painful moments of fear and hate, were far more common. The half-hour sessions drained me. It was slow progress. Each day I recovered a little faster, but it was never easy. It was even more difficult to read information from the emotions. That task was always secondary to keeping myself from unconsciousness. The most difficult emotions to control were those at the furthest ends of the spectrum—love and hate.

I didn't know who was projecting during the training sessions. I guessed that was for reasons of confidentiality. I was relieved not to know whom I was reading. It might be hard to sit at a meal with someone after being forced to share his or her most intense emotions.

"Let me check one more thing." Adric leaned out the doorway before returning. "Ready?"

"Ugh." I rolled my eyes. "Yeah." I stood in the middle of the empty room. A heavy, wool rug covered a portion of the floor. The strange black and white zigzag pattern was distracting. In earlier sessions, I closed my eyes to keep the pattern from causing a headache. A single chair hid in the farthest corner of the room.

A council member shouted from the hallway. "All good?"

Adric replied, "She's ready." His chest pressed against my back. "Bend the energy to your will." His hands rested on my shoulders grounding my body.

The hair on my arms stood on end. Energy flooded my system on a wave of charged air. It pushed, testing my strength. I imagined the force as a single thread and used my own emotional willpower to direct it in a path away from my body.

The energy mutated to a hue of black. It had an element of strength far greater than my own will. Blackness was something I'd feared since I was a child. My nightmares were plagued by it. I avoided dark rooms and empty buildings my whole life. I could think of nothing worse than being trapped by black energy.

"It's not working." My voice quivered.

Adric's breath was warm against my ear. "You can take the risk of bringing it in. The closer you allow it, the easier it is to bend. Remember, I can stop the exercise if it becomes too much."

I lured the hate-filled blackness closer. An image of a woman with long, blonde hair and tortoise-rimmed glasses emerged behind my closed lids. Tears raced down her face. Her dark green eyes flashed from sadness to sudden anger. A billowing green aura haloed her body before phasing to black. When the image cleared, I could see she was disheveled—hair now a wild mess of tangles and her clothes torn.

"I won't forget." Her cracked lips mouthed in silence.

Lunch soured in my stomach. I held a question in my mind: *What won't you forget?* I repeated it several times as I welcomed the energy closer little by little.

"Ione?" Adric's voice distracted me from my question. I'd been quiet for too long, frozen by the image in my mind and my efforts to interpret what I was witnessing.

I turned to face Adric. "I'm doing it. I can see so many things. And the energy—I'm holding it. But—"

His face broke into a smile.

My control faltered. The blackness slipped through my grip and struck. White-hot pain seared in my skull. I screamed.

"Stop the exercise!" Adric put one arm under my legs and scooped me up. The blackness dissipated. The pain stopped as suddenly as it started.

"Put me down." I pushed against his chest. "Damn it." Adric set me in the corner chair.

"What happened that time? You had it controlled." He bent to look me in the eye.

"Just...don't." I rubbed my eyes. "Nothing happened. I...got distracted. Will this Cyrus Reid guy be stronger than the volunteers?"

He hesitated. "I've talked it over with Alexander. There's no way to know for sure." He stood. "We're out of time"

"Hallelujah." I moved to stand. "It's been a long day. I'll be better after I sleep."

123

"No, Ione. I mean we leave tomorrow."

"What?" I shot up.

"We're fortunate we've had this much time." He said it with a sense of urgency I hadn't detected from him in the last several days. My heart sank.

"Tomorrow," I whispered.

"You aren't going anywhere alone." A weighted jacket of his emotions pressed against my body, determination and anxiety. "You should rest." He took two steps and paused in the doorway. "You're ready."

SIXTEEN

Simon Brown stood in the foyer, his sinewy frame clothed in black skinny jeans and an olive green T-shirt with white, block lettering that said WRD 2 YO MUTHA. His red Converse All-Star sneakers finished off his punk ensemble.

"Hello, dearie. I hear we're headed for the big bads. Going to be a shat show. Sure you're ready? By the way, I'm Simon. You can call me Big Daddy."

He winked one of his muddy brown eyes. His thick South African accent made everything he said intriguing, even if I didn't understand a word.

"Alright-y then. You stick with Simon. Save the Big Daddy talk for the bedroom." He was playful, but there was a charge in the air that hinted at apprehension.

The small chip in his upper right front tooth complimented his thin-lipped smile. It suited his snarky attitude and overflowing confidence. He put out his hand to shake mine. I placed my hand in his. He wrapped his arms around me, buried his face in my neck, and took in an exaggerated breath.

"You smell absolutely mouth-watering. What a delectable little biscuit."

I froze. He laughed and released his arms.

"Gotcha sweetness. You're fresh, aren't ya? I'm only playing. Though, if you want a go-round, you let me know." He winked again and wagged his brows. "Where're those two anyway? This train needs to leave the station. I like a braai much as the next bugger, just don't much care to be the biltong, ya know?"

I had no idea what he'd said.

Kali walked into the room. She was dressed in a simple set of black capris and a royal blue tunic blouse. Half her hair was pulled back at the crown of her head. She was peace embodied.

Desire and protective feelings floated from Simon's direction the moment she walked into the foyer. She stepped closer and a steam shower of affection humidified the room.

He was in love with her.

"'Bout time. Where's Captain America?" Simon played off his emotions as if they didn't exist.

I stared dumbfounded.

126

"Simon." Kali smiled as she kissed his cheek. "Adric will be here shortly. He's speaking with Alexander."

She stood next to me and placed her hand at the small of my back. "How are you feeling?"

"Fine."

I wanted to lean into her arm for a hug. She was bursting with warmth and concern. I fought not to crumple like a toddler. Her mothering aura was a tracker beam pulling me in.

"Bokkie, wanna tell your furry friend here to make room?" Simon motioned. Beo stood at my side blocking the only seat in the foyer. He'd struggled the past week with my training and was more attached than ever.

"Beo, come." I took several steps away from the bench. He moved with me and sat, touching my leg.

Simon slumped onto the bench and exemplified boredom. The front door opened, and Adric stood in the threshold.

"Captain America! Nice a'ya to join us…'bout damn time. Tell you what, I'll get the car, you load. My bags are already out front." Simon jumped up and walked out the door.

"Nice to see you too, Simon." Adric's voice was flat, his facial expression in opposition to his statement. "You two ready?" He looked at Kali, then at me.

"Yes. I've already taken my things to the vehicle. I'll go make sure Simon doesn't leave without us." Kali let out a quiet laugh.

Adric plucked my duffel bag from the floor. "Are *you* ready?"

"Sure." I gave him my best *are you crazy* face. He ignored it.

"Alexander's arranged for a private plane. It's a short flight. We'll be there in a couple of hours. Cyrus is in Colorado."

"Back to where we started. I'm happy to be closer to home." I paused, thinking. "On second thought, maybe it would be better if the big bad wasn't so close to home."

"The big bad? Simon's rubbing off already." Adric rolled his eyes.

"Just a touch, sweetness." I winked and sashayed out the door, leaving Adric laughing in the foyer.

We literally drove our car onto the tarmac at a private airstrip and loaded the plane. The jet was a fraction of the size of a normal passenger plane, but provided plenty of room for our few things and one unusually large wolf.

Adric spent the flight talking with the pilots. I put in my ear buds, turned up the volume, and composed a message to Jenny on my phone. I didn't know what was going to happen when we arrived in Denver. The prospect of things going badly, coupled with my guilt, caused an urgent tightening in my chest.

I stared at the blinking cursor. Whatever I said, it had to be the truth.

I'm on my way to Colorado. I'll let you know where I'm at when I get settled. I'll call you tonight. We need to talk. I have a lot to tell you.

> *XOXO,*
> *Ione*

I hit send before I had a chance to chicken out. Ending an email with *We need to talk. I have a lot to tell you*, was code for *shit is going to get real*.

A vehicle was waiting for us on the airstrip when we landed. Fifteen-minutes in a sedan headed south delivered us to another of Alexander's homes.

Even in the shadowy pre-dawn, I could see the house was a monstrosity. The towering Tudor-style manor sat in the center of a sprawling lawn. An imposing eight-foot masonry fence surrounded the house.

The multitude of imprinted antiques inside comforted me as we walked through the double-door entrance. Everything in the house with an imprint was haloed in a *good* color—lemon yellows and tangerines. It would take more than a few warm and fuzzy antiques to convince me Alexander wasn't bad news.

I found my room and unpacked a few things. Beo asked to go outside as soon as I'd finished.

The lawns surrounding the property weren't as manicured as those in Chicago, but the view of the

Rockies was far more appealing than anything in Illinois. I soaked in the familiarity of the mountains.

I felt Adric before I heard his footfalls behind me. His standard emotional imprint had become a sensation I recognized.

"Where does all of Alexander's money come from?" I asked. "This house, and the one in Chicago, each are worth several million dollars. A private flight? It seems excessive."

Adric wasn't surprised by the question. His emotions were calm and even, his status quo emotional state. "Alexander was married once. His wife was an exceptionally powerful Omni." I opened my mouth. He stopped me. "The myths about oracles are based on Omnis." I closed my jaw. "Most are effective at predicting the future, but their predictions are specific, not universal." His arms folded across his chest. "Some use their abilities to improve their own station in life. Others share their talents. Josephine was more of the former." He shrugged. "She was able to predict with acute accuracy global financial markets. She and Alexander made a fortune investing as venture capitalists."

"Are they divorced?"

"She died." Adric looked to the east horizon, checking the progress of the creeping sun.

"How?"

"An accidental overdose." He gave a one-shouldered shrug. "It's not uncommon for Omnis to use substances to help deal with the side effects of their visions." He unfolded his arms. "Alexander was heartbroken."

I wasn't sure I believed Alexander had the capacity to be heartbroken, but then again, maybe her death was what made him that way. "What's the difference between an Omni and a Seer?"

He shuffled one boot against the gavel. "Omnis see flashes of the future. What you see is tied to emotion. And…you can manipulate it."

I laughed. "I'm just trying to avoid Sleeping Beauty Syndrome every time I'm in a room full of revved-up people. *Manipulate* is a little too suggestive, don't you think?"

"No."

A rush of heat shot through me. "I guess we'll have to agree to disagree."

"Don't underestimate your ability." His stern voice left no room for argument. He turned to walk back to the house. "I'm going to get some work done and catch a short nap. We'll meet in the dining room in—" Adric glanced at his watch, "—four hours. Get some rest. You'll need it."

He didn't wait for my response. The door slammed shut. He had not spoken to me on the flight. Now he'd taken off with a quick dismissal and a bossy command to rest. I knew his behavior was part of Tracker Adric work mode. He made the switch the moment we loaded in the car and headed for the airport in Chicago.

131

Still, I couldn't help the swell of anger that bubbled when I heard the door close. I was nervous about what was to come. I missed Jenny, and now my tether in all this strangeness was being an ass.

It was childish to be angry, but the energy bouncing through my head like a hundred different rubber balls was too much.

It would be best to try and rest, but sleep would be elusive. I'd likely lie in bed wide-awake and think. Only one thing helped when I couldn't turn off my brain.

I was back downstairs in my running gear in less than ten minutes. I grabbed a piece of paper and a pen from the small antique desk near the door.

> *Went for a run with Beo. Be back before meeting.*
> *Have my phone. Call if you need me.*
> *-Ione*

I slipped out of the house and into the sunlight. I looked up a route on my phone. I wanted to stay off the beaten path and out of any populated neighborhoods. I couldn't risk someone reporting a wolf loose in a south Denver suburb. There was a green belt connecting to a reservoir area behind the property.

I double-checked the route, selected my playlist, jammed my ear buds in, and tucked my phone into my sports bra. I was off the property, finding a steady pace before the first song change.

I let my mind go. I didn't think about what was to come, and I wasted no time or energy questioning if I was ready. I *escaped*.

I listened to my breathing and the steady music pounding in my ears. I found a small game trail leading to the reservoir. As usual, Beo trotted out in front of me, happy to be running.

The sun was warm. The wind was absent, and the rolling hills and tall grass made a beautiful frame around the reservoir in the distance. I'd covered over two miles before my legs began to tire.

I slowed when I noticed Beo running back to me in an all-out sprint. I pulled at my headphones. A gunshot rang out splitting open the silence. In what felt like the same moment, I was tackled from behind.

SEVENTEEN

The bones in my face cracked with the initial contact against the ground. My knees followed suit, with the right side taking the brunt of the combined weight of my body and the behemoth of man who tackled me.

As my face dragged against the loose rocks of the path, my first layer of flesh was left behind. My eyes filled with dirt and debris, and instantly watered. I flailed, trying to resist the momentum carrying us downhill. The tangy metallic taste of blood exploded on my tounge.

I opened my mouth only to take in more dust. He'd knocked the wind out of me. I gulped and swallowed mouthfuls of soil before my lungs finally filled with air. We stopped moving. The man was on my back. His hot breath melted into the stinging flesh of the side of my face.

"Gotcha." He reeked of alcohol and cigarettes. He reached for my waist and began tugging at my pants. "Well, aren't you a sweet young thing. Little fun before I bring you in won't hurt."

I shrieked. He clutched his calloused hand over my mouth. His fat fingers smelled like boiled onions and smoke. The stench made me gag, and I coughed.

He rubbed the length of his body against me and ground his hips into my backside. I bit at his hand, twisted, and tried to attain leverage.

The ground beneath us stripped more of my already tender skin each time I fought against him. Adrenaline fueled my panic and dulled the pain. With my one free hand, I reached for his hair and eyes.

"Hold still, little bitch! I always liked a fighter, but you just let it happen, you hear."

The coarse skin of his hand pushed up against the bottom of my nose. The meat of his palm covered my mouth.

I slowed when breathing became difficult. His emotions had a telltale intensity I'd come to know. He was Vryzoldak.

His arousal was thick—anticipation underlined by a need for violence. He stretched for my waist and slid his hand into my panties. "Atta girl. I'll get my fill and then get you back."

Fingers pushed against the inside of my thigh as he tugged my clothes farther down to my knees. The intense fear that raked through me ignited a second wind.

The hand covering my mouth slipped. I caught one of his fingers between my lips. My teeth sunk into the tissue. Warm blood ran into the back of my throat. It gurgled with my desperate breathing.

He yelled something into my ear and hooked his fingers into my cheek. My neck caught the torque of his pull. Piercing pain ran down my spine. The thin skin at the corner of my mouth tore. I choked on the mixture of blood, dirt, and his thick digits filling my mouth. My gag reflex kicked in. I vomited.

The man yelled again, "You stupid bitch!" He released my mouth. I could breathe.

His club of a hand slammed down across the side of my head. The impact was numbing. My head bounced off the ground.

I heard the agonized whelp of a wild animal. I realized the noise had come from me. My eyes lulled into the back of my head and fogginess settled into my brain.

Enraged snarls filled my ears. The sounds were both terrifying and heavenly at once. Shouting from the man. A weight lifted. I could move.

My eyes were full of dirt, swollen from irritation and the impact of my face breaking my fall.

My vision was darkened and blurry. The landscape circled around me. I attempted to stand and stumbled, clambering to the ground. A knife-like pain ran through my leg as I fell and tumbled down a steep rocky hill. I could hear my attacker's muffled screams interspersed with Beo's snarls.

When I slowed, I tried to stand but couldn't make it to my feet. My pants were still around my ankles. I pulled at them. My swollen hands couldn't hold the fabric. I crawl-walked as far from the sounds as I could. My sight returned. I could identify fuzzy outlines of the ground and horizon. I stood, tugging my pants up as much as possible. I didn't know where I was going, but as long as the sounds were farther and farther away, I knew I was heading in the right direction.

My pants were torn, and the cloth that remained was soaked in blood. My right knee ruptured in pain with each step. I'd worn a fitted long-sleeve running shirt that was drenched with dripping blood from by nose and teeth. Rocks and dirt were embedded in my hands and forearms.

I found a hidden spot under a group of pine trees that crowded the lake. I removed my shirt and used the material to help clean out my eyes. My hands and face were tender. Skin hung in spots, exposing the thin layer of fat just above the bone. The soft cotton of my running shirt was like sandpaper. I bent down to the water at the edge of the reservoir and wet the fabric.

The damp material helped to clean my eyes. The frigid water was instead boiling hot on my stinging skin. I cired, and my entire body shook with each sob.

I surveyed the hill I'd fallen down. I couldn't locate Beo or the attacker. I reached into my bra to retrieve my phone.

It was gone.

My body trembled.

Noise from behind stanched my quivering. I clutched a rock from the ground and turned to bludgeon whoever was there.

Beo materialized in the alcove. He stopped and stared. His face, chest, and both front legs were painted in blood. I ran my hands over his body. He dropped his head and flinched a whine when my fingers hovered over his left flank. I separated the blood-matted fur.

"Oh, God!" The raspy gurgle I heard didn't sound like my voice.

Heat from a bullet had burned his skin and scorched his hair. I couldn't tell if it had gone in or only grazed his body.

I collapsed to the ground, shuddering with howling cries. I lay at the side of the reservoir until Beo began to nuzzle me. I wiggled into my bloody dirt-encrusted shirt and stood. My whole body screamed in resistance. I had to favor my right knee. I could only manage a hunched position, but I could move. I calculated which direction I'd come from and put one foot in front of the other.

I recognized where I was tackled after what seemed like a lifetime of limping, tripping uphill, and crawling in spots. Blood and shreds of clothing littered the hillside. When I was closer, I realized it wasn't just bits of fabric, but pieces of skin and tissue. The sight and stench of my own vomit from earlier took me over the edge. I heaved.

My body convulsed with each spasm. I shook with weakness and the effects of shock. Beo came close, and I pulled myself up by gripping his fur and leaning into his considerable body. Standing, I could see where Beo dragged the man.

He was lying on his front with his face turned back to me. He'd been pulled about ten feet on the downslope side of the trail. One of his arms was twisted backward, partly detached from his body, and more than half of his face resembled raw hamburger. His throat had been chewed through.

There was nothing left in my stomach, but my body reacted to the carnage with revulsion. Every fiber of my being urged me to turn and run.

The man was dead, and if someone was with him, he would've found me by now. I had to try to find something to use to identify him.

As Beo and I approached, I did what I could to avoid looking at the man's face. Only because it was attached to the front of his head would someone have known the mottled pile of blood and tissue was human. I silently prayed he'd been stupid enough to carry ID.

My prayers were answered when my shaking fingers made their way into his back pocket and touched the soft, palpable leather of a wallet. I pinched it between my fingers and tugged it free. I crawled up the hill faster than I would have thought possible.

As I made it back onto the small game trail, I could see a glimmer of something black and metallic in the sagebrush.

I stuffed the wallet down my sports bra and stooped as far as my body would allow. I'd hoped what I'd seen was my phone. Instead, I found myself staring at the butt of a gun. My heart raced.

I pulled it free from the bush and brought it close to my face so I could see it with my battered eyes. I could barely make out the GLOCK logo on the bottom of the handle. The magazine that was full of ammunition when I checked.

If jackass number one had someone who came looking for him, I had two weapons at my disposal. They both packed a nasty bite. I willed myself to continue walking.

The approximate 2.5 miles I'd managed before being tackled was traversed in less than thirty mintues. I struggled for two hours to limp that distance back.

The impassable brick wall taunted me as I approached the house. I hobbled all the way around to the front of the property. As I limped closer to the house, the possibility dawned that whoever attacked me may have also attacked the house.

A live wire of fear jolted through me. The thought of Adric, Simon, and Kali under attack shocked me into alertness.

I approached as quietly as my stiff limbs would allow. I loaded a bullet into the chamber of the gun I held in my mangled hands and attempted to extend my arms. Beo stayed tucked in close, keeping me upright. I'd been leaning on him for at least the last mile. With both hands extended, I had even more difficulty walking. Beo did what he could to help.

The swelling in my face had worsened in the time spent traveling back to the house. If I had to shoot, it would require a miracle for the bullet to find its intended target.

The front door flew open, and I moved my finger to the trigger.

"Stop!" I didn't recognize my own voice.

"Sweet Mallie Mary! You look like a white walker!"

Simon's voice. I dropped the gun and crumpled into a pile on the lawn.

141

EIGHTEEN

I woke to Kali sitting beside my bed. I was acutely aware of every scrape, bruise, bump, sprain, and break I'd sustained. I couldn't move with ease, and fought to breathe. My eyelids felt as if they protruded past my nose.

"You're awake!" Kali held a glass of water. "Drink. It'll help your throat."

I urged my sore arms toward the cup. The tug of an IV in my left forearm restrained my movement, and I realized my hands were covered in bandages. Kali put the glass to my lips. The water was difficult to swallow but did help my burning throat.

"Beo?" I attempted a whisper. It sounded garbled.

"He's fine. We're keeping him separate from you to protect the doctor." She stood and opened the bedroom door. "She's awake."

A lanky man walked into the room. He wore a pair of khaki slacks and a light blue oxford shirt. A stethoscope hung around his neck. His wire-rimmed glasses framed somewhat familiar brown eyes. Wrinkles bordering his eyes and mouth were etched into dark brown skin. I recognized him from somewhere, but my thoughts were difficult to focus.

The man stood close, and his nearness had a calming effect. I closed my eyes, taking in the sensation. He had a unique scent, something like chamomile and peppermint.

"Hello, Ms. McCreery. I'm Wayne Mullins." He pushed his glasses up the bridge of his nose. "I'm a physician. I specialize in treating hybrids and elites. Adric called me as soon as you were found. I've treated your injuries to the extent possible. I've done what I can until you regained consciousness. I'd like to talk to you about your attack if you are comfortable enough to do so."

I wouldn't be comfortable for months. *Mullins?* My foggy brain worked on putting something together.

"Where's Adric?" I croaked.

Kali left the room and closed the door. Dr. Mullins sat in the chair she'd been using. Being alone in a room with a stranger sent a rush of fear through me.

"I've asked Adric to allow me to speak to you alone. We stepped outside the room just before you regained consciousness." He sighed. "Ms. McCreery, I did a thorough assessment of your injuries, but I didn't check to determine if you've been sexually assaulted. Ms. Gupta asked that I wait for your permission. Is that particular exam necessary?"

His voice, while deep and resounding, was calm. I was the emotional energy equivalent of Valium. I could tell he wasn't Vryzoldak. Vryzoldak emotions drenched my senses by the bucketful. Dr. Mullins' aura reminded me of wading in cool water.

"No." I shuddered, thinking about how close I'd come to what he suggested.

"Ms. McCreery. I'd like—"

"Ione...call me Ione."

He flashed a concerned smile. "Ione, I'd like to ask your permission to administer an unusually specialized medication. It isn't something I do lightly, but given the circumstances, it's the best course of treatment."

He watched me to be sure I was following. I attempted to nod.

"This is an intravenous form of medication made from the concentrated formulation of an intracellular antioxidant enzyme found in Vryzoldak blood plasma. This enzyme activates the healing process." He paused. "It allows for quick tissue repair.

It aids in an unusually fast recovery of your wounds. However, there are side effects."

"What…" I attempted to swallow "…are the side effects?"

"With the high dosage necessary, they are extensive. They may include delusions and visual hallucinations. The physical effects include sweating, nausea, increased heart rate and blood pressure, sleeplessness, and possible tremors. You may also suffer impaired depth and time perception, with distorted perception of the size and shape of objects, movements, color, sound, touch, and your own body image. This may all be heightened because of your abilities as a Seer." He shifted in his seat "Sensations may seem to give you the feeling of hearing colors and seeing sounds. These changes can be frightening. You could also experience severe, terrifying thoughts and feelings, fear of losing control, fear of insanity, and if not closely monitored, death."

My mind was slow and groggy. *Death?* "I'm not going to die from my road rash." I struggled to say so many words.

"I want you to fully understand the consequences of using this medication. It'll heal you in less than an hour of real time. However, that hour may seem like days to you once the side effects begin." He continued.

"Ione, you've suffered from a significant concussion. Your right knee will require surgery. Your hands will need skin graphs to heal properly. You have several broken ribs, a broken nose, and other small fractures in your face. There are also breaks in many of your fingers and metatarsals. I can't be sure without taking x-rays, but I believe your skull has a hairline fracture. I'm not going to mention the countless deep bone contusions. It'll take months for you to recover without exceptional aid." He paused, contemplating something. "There is something else you don't know. There's been another attack."

My heart stopped in my chest.

"Ten more bodies were found…Vryzoldak children."

A flash of heat swept through my body. "When?" My voice cracked.

"Not long after your attack."

Scorching shame seethed into me. Had I not made the ridiculously stupid mistake that led to my attack, there was a chance we could've found something to stop the attack. Hot tears spilled over my swollen lids and ran down my cheeks.

"There was nothing to be done about it." Dr. Mullins leaned closer. "Adric believes he's tracked Cyrus' location, but that development is new. There was no warning, no way of stopping it. The next one…" He paused and waited for me to make eye contact. "Perhaps it can be stopped. But right now, we're waiting on you. How many more deaths might there be in the six months it would take for you to heal?" He shook his head. "I've weighed the options, and I don't make this recommendation lightly. I'm confident I can titrate the drug to control the speed of metabolism and guarantee your safety."

I attempted a deep breath. Shooting pain pierced my chest. "Can I talk to Adric?"

Dr. Mullins nodded. As he stood to go, I remembered where I'd seen him.

"They interviewed you after the attack at the Olympic center."

He nodded. "I'm the primary physician for many of the athletes who were killed at the training facility."

His sorrow pooled around me, a delicate drowning of emotion.

"I'm sorry," I said, knowing it wasn't enough.

He nodded again, and without speaking, he left the room.

Adric peered in. "My God," he whispered.

The expression of horror plastered across his face was indication enough of how he felt—and I looked. Worse was the fury he couldn't block. His anger was a poorly concealed explosive ready to detonate at any moment.

"More like zombie apocalypse, Captain." Simon and Kali walked in behind Adric. "Our lil' Sacajawea looks like something I might pull from the crisper six months after it's past its prime. Shat! You look like...well, shat." Simon's jab was a welcome distraction form Adric's acidic anger.

"Simon, please, a little consideration for her feelings," Kali scolded.

"I'd like to speak to Ione alone." Adric hadn't taken his eyes off me.

After expressing they were relived to see me alive and awake—Kali far more elegantly than Simon, the two left the room.

Nerves stirred in my belly as Adric moved closer. I couldn't ignore his emotional response, and I knew it was warranted.

He sat in the chair near the bed. His hands fisted in his lap. I couldn't wait any longer for him to speak.

"Is Beo okay?"

"Yes." A single word—abrupt and cold, was all he said.

"It was a stupid mistake." My gravelly voice cracked.

Adric looked at me agonized. He shook his head and ran his fingers through his hair. I stared at my bandaged hands.

"My God, Ione." He brought his hands down to his lap with force.

I flinched.

His anger dissipated so quickly it left the room feeling like a vacuum.

"I'm sorry," he said softly, as he inched away. "I don't…I mean…" He pursed his lips. "I hate that I can't touch you and know that you're okay."

I stared at him, taking in the full breadth of agony in his blue eyes. He wasn't angry with me, he was angry *at what happened to me.*

148

"I'm not angry with you for running. Maybe I was, but I'm not now." He sighed. "Unless you were running away and not just running." He paused. "That's different."

He was struggling to choose his words and holding back tears. I stared at the window across the room, uneasy with the idea of seeing him cry.

"The doctor says he has something that will fix it. I mean, me—fix me."

"I wanted to be alone with you so I could make sure you're comfortable taking the Juice. You don't have to do it. It's excruciating, and no one knows exactly what it'll do to you."

"Juice? What a cliché name."

Adric chuckled. He drew his chair closer. I could smell a blend of fresh air and his signature mixture of cloves and leather.

"You're so beaten up. I hardly recognize you."

"It'll be okay." My words fell short of convincing.

"I've lost my sister, so many friends and even more acquaintances. If you…" He paused. "I'm not sure I could take it." He shifted uncomfortably in the small chair. His pain vibrated against my tender skin.

"I know what it's like to lose your family. You don't ever get used to it. You just start to have a new normal after a while."

Being reminded of my dad's loss, compounded with Adric's emotions, was like reliving

149

his death. A deluge of briny tears poured from my eyes. They fell without sound, without effort, an underwater spring of sorrow uncorked from somewhere within me.

Adric cradled my tender body with calculated effort.

The contact was permission to release everything I'd been trying so hard to contain—rage, fear, shame, relief. They rolled through me with violence.

We stayed folded into each other until my eyes were dry. Adric carefully pulled away and laid me on the bed.

"Are you okay?" His hands continued to caress my forearms.

"Yes…and no." My voice was all but gone. "It's blurry." The memory of a mutilated face sprinted through my mind. I shuddered and swallowed back bile.

"I can tell you a few things." He wiped at a tear clinging to my chin. "Beo is fine. A bullet grazed him, but it only took a few stiches to repair. He's as good as new." Adric huffed. "He wasn't easy to treat. We had to use a tranquilizer. And he's nearly eaten through the cage we've been keeping him in."

I blanched at the idea of him caged.

"We've been taking good care of him." Adric held my hands in his. "The man who attacked you is dead—Jeremy Hitland. He's Crestere. Do you remember? You brought back his wallet."

I nodded. I remembered. I'd never forget his half-eaten face. I blinked several times.

"Going back for the wallet—that was brave…and stupid."

I met his eyes. "I know," I croaked.

"It's a miracle you made it all the way back to the house, considering the shape you were in." He leaned toward me and brushed hair from my face. His hand on my tender skin left a trail of warmth. "Are you sure you're ready for this?"

He was talking about the medicine, but I couldn't help wondering if his question meant more. I was more ready for the Juice than what might happen afterward, assuming my body would heal.

"They know about me." Pain wracked my body. I groaned.

"Hey, whoa." Adric ran his fingers over my hair. "You're safe."

I closed my eyes. "I'm *not* safe."

"We don't know if you were attacked because they know who you are a Seer, or if it was a coincidence—because you were traveling with us." His voice was clipped and professional. He'd transitioned into Tracker Adric.

I pinned him with bloodshot eyes. "Don't." I couldn't stand his tone. "You don't think it was a coincidence, and neither do I." I rolled my head on the pillow and closed my eyes again.

Pain demanded my attention, but there was one more question I needed answered.

"Why are you waiting? If you know where he's at, why not go without me?" My question hung in the air ignored. "Adric?" I turned my head.

"Alexander gave express instructions that *you* are to speak with Cyrus."

I had a strong disliking for Alexander Odin. My aversion grew. "Why?" My voice was shot. I spoke in a scratchy whisper. My parched throat was swollen like the rest of me. I coughed and pain doubled in my chest.

"Listen, right now, just worry about getting better. Are you sure about the Juice?"

If whatever Dr. Mullins was going to give me would make the excruciating pain in my body subsist, I wanted it—no matter what the short-lived side effects might be. I nodded, and even that hurt.

"I'll send in Dr. Mullins." Adric bent and kissed my forehead.

When I opened my eyes, he'd already made it to the door. I stared at my bandaged hands and thought of what I'd escaped. I shuddered remembering the attack. *The attack I'd survived.*

I'd been hunted like an unsuspecting animal in an open field. If I was going to manage any level of success with Cyrus Reid, I was going to have to pull my head out of my ass.

NINETEEN

A stinging at the center of my chest slowly intensified. Heat rolled out from my belly toward my back and down my limbs. A thick, black liquid crept over my skin, pooling at my chest, abdomen, and the palms of my hands. I screamed. My eyes peeled open as if my lids were glued shut. In the center of my chest was a single blackened handprint. Bubbling charred skin cracked and bled.

Snow swirled. Tiny razor-sharp pieces of ice raged against my bare body. I curled in on myself. Cuts in my back tore open as I brought my knees to my chest and huddled my shoulders. I bellowed in pain.

A soundless stream of violet currents rushed from my lips as my joints were pulled in opposing directions. My back *splayed open, skin peeling back into itself. Something grew out of the opened skin. Oversized black talons sprouted from the ends of my fingers. They dug into the mixture of mud and melting snow below my convulsing body. The soil released trickles of crimson blood. I scrambled to move away from the hemorrhaging dirt.*

I was no longer myself. My skin was rubbery, black, leather. Enormous obsidian wings rested against my spine.

The converging streams of blood oozing from the ground formed an expanding pool of liquid. My charred feet sunk into the river of red. As I plunged into the liquid, the weight of my wings pulled me deeper. I could neither resist the pull, nor the pressure building in my lungs. I inhaled. My scorched throat filled with the tangy wetness of blood.

Darkness approached. Blissfully, I felt nothing.

"Ione? Can you hear me?"

"You sound half mad you crazy bugger. Can you hear me? She's just ignoring you. Try something like… 'Sweetness, I bought you a new pair of El Gringo boots, these without any rank horse shat. You have three seconds to wake up, or I'm keepin' 'em.'"

Only one person called me sweetness.

"I'm holding you to that promise." My voice was normal. Much to my surprise, my vision was perfect. I pushed myself up.

Adric sat nearby. Dr. Mullins stood on my opposite side, monitoring a machine hooked up to my arm. Simon and Kali stood at the bottom of the bed staring back at me.

"Ah, my little Pocahontas, I didn't promise a thing—but I did get you to open your eyes."

I smiled. "I thought I was Sacajawea?"

"Oh, right. Well, bokkie, keep up the sass and I'll start calling ya Princess Talkstoomuch. Glad you're all healed up, Sweetness. I have things to get to. I'll meet you all—the motley part of the crew—downstairs in a bit." He winked and meandered to the door.

I inhaled a breath of pure vibrancy. He was right. I was healed. It was freaking weird, but it worked.

"How do you feel, Ione?" Dr. Mullins immediately had my attention.

"I feel incredible."

"Physiologically, you handled the medication well. I was able to give you far less than planned. You were only under for about forty-five minutes." Dr. Mullins walked around the bed and stood next to Adric. "I want to check out a few things—draw some blood and look over your injuries. But, assuming you're as well as I think you are, you can all be on your way soon." He smiled. "Excuse us, please."

Everyone else headed for the door. Just before ducking out, Adric smiled and winked. He looked nothing like Simon when he did it. His jaw flexed as he pinched his right eye closed. One side of his mouth rose as the muscles of his face contracted. I winked back.

Dr. Mullins inspected my body, paying particular attention to my heart and lungs. I was relieved to see I didn't have a charred black handprint scarring the center of my chest. The memory of the hallucinations and the pain of the healing process flashed through my mind. A wave of nausea hit me.

"Everything alright?" Dr. Mullins stopped his poking and prodding.

"I'm fine." I took a deep breath and reminded myself I *was* fine. I was more than fine. "Will it last? This high or whatever it is. I feel invincible."

"You're tapering off the endorphin high. It'll be another several hours before you're back to normal. I assure you, you're not invincible. Your wounds are healed, and barring any new injuries, you'll remain that way."

"This drug, it's not something that's readily available?" I met Dr. Mullins's brown eyes. He knew what I was insinuating. He stopped moving.

"It's more dangerous than it's worth in many ways. For one, it's highly addictive. This high you're feeling now, it will fade. It takes more and more of the drug, with each exposure, to achieve the previous high—and the previous healing effect. Second, patients must be closely monitored during administration. Even the slightest mistake in dosage can prove fatal. Not all people can handle the psychological side effects. Those who can withstand the drug often never recover from what they see on the other side of the coma. I'll talk with you more about that later. And there is the exposure of the entire Vryzoldak race to think about. What of their safety? Their blood is what allows for the creation of the drug. There's a fine line between utilizing a gift and exploiting a resource."

He shifted his attention to my arm and removed my IV. When he moved, I watched the small puncture heal in a single second.

"Whoa!"

"Yes, it's quite remarkable," he added.

Dr. Mullins's emotions were stronger than I'd sensed the last time we were together. The warmth of his emotional imprint was able to reach deep inside my body, as if it could actually warm my bones.

"What are you? You don't read like a Vryzoldak or a regular human."

"I don't?" He was surprised. "How so?" He tilted his head. His intelligent eyes were focused with obvious curiosity. I was suddenly nervous about describing it.

"Well, Vryzoldak emotions are strong— intense when they're not guarded. Yours are subtle. I can read you, but you also give off a warm, almost numbing, sensation that feels…well, it feels *really* good." I felt my cheeks flush.

He smiled. "Interesting. I'm what we call a Phamak. For your understanding, the closest thing you might equate would be a shaman."

"You're a healer."

"I try." He smiled, his face suddenly much younger looking. "I'm pleased the treatment worked. I believe you're ready to go. I'll double-check some labs after I run them through my computer." He patted my shoulder. "It's a relief to see you well, young lady."

"Wait." He stopped. "Does Juice heal the brain? I mean, can it heal your memory?" Dr. Mullins squinted in confusion.

"I can't remember anything farther back than about eleven years ago. I'd always thought it was amnesia. Maybe some kind of brain trauma I'd experienced as a young child."

"It's possible. I haven't spent any time studying it myself. What is the earliest memory you are able to recall right now?"

A jolt of hope shot through me. "Um..." I closed my eyes. Like a movie in rewind, I started to reverse my life. The tape stopped. I shook my head. "Nothing. I remember my dad standing in the doorway of our house. I see his back, the outline of his cowboy hat backlit by the sun. It's the same thing I always see when I try to remember my childhood."

He patted my shoulder, "I'll see what I can find. Be patient. It may take time."

"Thanks for everything you've done."

"You're welcome." He slipped out the door.

Adric peeked in. "We're hoping to leave in an hour. There's something we need to check out. Can you be ready?"

I ran my fingers through my hair. "I'd like to shower first. Otherwise, I'm good to go. Oh, and brush my teeth. Hey, will you send in Beo? I'd like to see him."

As soon as I said his name, the giant beast pounced into the room. He was on the bed in a single leap and licking my face from chin to forehead. He plunged his enormous head against my chest and groaned as he burrowed against me. He flopped onto his back. I scratched behind his ears and rubbed his belly with unabashed affection.

The dreadful memory of taking the Juice was only an echo in my mind. The high I was riding steamrolled the memory. My body buzzed with energy. The muscles of my face were tight with the ridiculousness of my perma-grin.

"You're all better, buddy!" I grazed my fingers over his stiches. The injury was almost healed. "Exactly how long was I out?"

Adric ran one hand over his chin scruff. "After the attack, you were unconscious for four days. Dr. Mullins sedated you. He was convinced you had brain swelling. There were several times he considered having you transferred to a hospital, but area hospitals aren't secure. He knew he couldn't administer Juice anywhere but here. It was a long four days. If you'd taken any longer to come to, he would've been forced to make the decision about treatment without your consent." He took a deep breath. "By the way, I found something of yours." He reached into his pocket and tossed me my cell phone. The backside of the phone was shattered. "I think it will still work just needs a charge."

"Four days. Jenny! She's going to kill me when she finds out I'm alive." My heart drummed in my chest. I couldn't control the energy effervescing inside my body. "God, I feel like I'm going to burst into flames!"

Adric laughed, and sat next to me on the bed. "About earlier." He paused. "I'm sorry. You're right. I don't think the attack was a coincidence. I—"

"When I woke up, you were the first person I wanted to see." I reached up to put my hands on either side of his face. The warm, rough texture of his facial hair under my palms was soothing. His eyes pulled me closer, and I leaned in. I pressed my lips against his.

He brought intensity to the kiss. My body quivered with waves of arousal we were both creating. His arms slammed our bodies together. I opened my mouth wider. He did the same.

His guard crumbled. Emotions flooded my senses with hot need. Heat pounded through me. I opened my mind, pulling his emotions in and releasing the hold I had on my own.

He stopped.

I fought the urge to crawl on top of him and force him to continue kissing me. The compounding of our matching emotions was intoxicating.

"You projected."

"What?" My voice matched his, labored with heavy breath.

"Some Seers have the ability to project, but I'd never imagined what it might feel like." He smiled.

We had separated a little. I realized the moment was passing and slouched against my pillows. "Add projecting to the growing list of bizarre things I can do."

He brought his face down to mine and kissed me with tenderness our previous entanglement was missing. He pulled away so we could see one another.

"Is that what it's like for you all the time? Is that how everyone else's emotions feel?"

I thought about the intoxicating blend of our emotions. "No." I raised a single brow. "Is that what it's like for you all the time?"

"No." His lips were on mine.

We parted when we both required air. Everywhere he touched me, a trail of charged force followed. He kissed a path from my ear down my neck to my collarbone. I arched my back encouraging him. I gasped when his hands ran from my knees, up my thighs, and grazed by hips.

I froze.

My mind flashed back to the field near the reservoir. "Stop!" He was off me instantly. "I'm sorry…I can't do this."

"It's all right. I understand." Adric put his arms around me and sat us both up on the bed. "Shhh." He rested his cheek on the top of my head.

161

"I'm sorry… It wasn't you. I was back there."

"It's okay."

"I'd made it up in my mind it was over. I'd decided I'd won."

"It's not that easy."

We sat in silence for several seconds.

"Thank you," I said.

He let out a sardonic laugh. "For what? Dragging you into this nightmare?"

I pushed away so I could see him. I could feel his regret—cold and stinging on my skin.

"I'm by far the most disappointed this happened the way it did, but you can't take all the credit."

He looked away.

I pulled his face to mine and stared into his eyes, willing him to see things my way—to allow me to take blame for my own mistake. Icy regret continued to tangle his emotions. My temper flared. "Damn it, Adric. I'm not helpless, and I'm not your sister."

He pushed my hand from his face. His guard went up, walling me out from his emotions. Frustration welled inside my chest. "We're supposed to be helping *each other*. So quit your bullshit self-loathing about dragging me along. I came willingly. I could've said no and stayed in Cattle Creek—maybe I should've. It's too late now."

I crawled over him, straddling his lower body between my legs. His guard was up, he could try to hide, but I wouldn't give in.

Adric stared at me in silence, and I stared back.

I wasn't ready when his wall came down. I sucked in a shocked breath as his emotions were released at full throttle. A deep ache of grief followed by a throbbing undertone of pain gripped my chest. I grunted. He grabbed my waist, steadying my body as he pushed his emotions at me with eagerness. More powerful than the grief was a suffocating fear. It crept over my skin in a poisonous fog. I drew in another breath through clenched teeth and dug my fingers into the muscles of his shoulders.

He was terrified that if the Crestere succeed in finding me—and they'd come dangerously close, he would lose the only thing left in the world he cared about.

When our eyes met, I let myself crash into him. My lips pressed against his. I poured my feelings for him back into his body—the attraction, the gratitude, connection, and depth of safety I felt with him.

His body relaxed under mine. The kiss softened. I pulled away, and his energy ebbed. I let go of the stream of emotion he'd given me. It escaped my grasp like water running through my fingers.

He rested his forehead against mine. "It's never been like that for me." One corner of his mouth pulled into a half smile.

I lowered my face and kissed his lopsided grin.

TWENTY

We loaded into a navy blue SUV. Adric drove, I took the passenger seat, and Kali and Simon sat in the second row seats. The cargo area of the vehicle held Beo and a collection of various supplies hidden in oversized black plastic cases.

Simon was along for more than just crooning over Kali. He was an ace at computers—a hacker by trade. He'd used Jeremy Hitland's credit cards to track his recent whereabouts. The information helped Adric narrow his search. We were doing recon now in the hope of pinpointing a headquarters or hideout for Cyrus and the Crestere.

I recognized where we were headed. I'd driven this highway before, going to Red Rocks Amphitheater. Morrison, Colorado seemed a strange place for the Crestere to hide.

My phone chimed to life.

"It works!" I hit Adric's shoulder with excitement.

My relief was short-lived. I had no messages or texts from Jenny. I confirmed the email I'd sent her the day of the attack had been delivered. I called her number twice—nothing. On the third call, I left a message.

Jenny, call me. I need to talk to you. It's important. Love you.

I glanced at Adric to see if he'd heard me. He was distracted.

I called Jenny's mom—no answer. "Shit!" I tossed my phone onto the console. It clattered into the back seat and dangled by the cord.

Kali handed it to me. "I haven't told you why I decided to join this assignment. Would you like to know?"

I turned in my chair. She was beautiful, as always, if a bit more daring. Her hair was pulled back and pinned in a bun at the base of her skull. She wore a fitted long-sleeved shirt and leather pants. She was in black from her hair to her steel-toed boots.

I adjusted in my seat to face her.

"I was married once. My husband, Navrang knew me better than I knew myself, but that was to be expected." She paused. "He was a Seer, like you."

"What?" The question escaped my lips without permission.

She smiled. "Well, not exactly like you. His mutation was weak. He could read me, but I don't know if that was his Sight or his heart." She smiled again at the memory. "He couldn't control emotion, but he did have a companion. Not all Seers are strong enough to keep one. Rajan was a wonderful protector. She lived with us for many years. She died protecting our children."

I swallowed hard, guessing where this story might go.

"Navrang was a target, like all Seers. Back then, there were only a few remaining, and he'd stayed well hidden for years. When the Crestere discovered he was a Seer, they murdered my family—Navrang, our son, our infant daughter, and Rajan. They made it appear as a car accident, but it was no accident." Tension struck my body as her emotions ran through me. "I would have been satisfied to join them, but the Crestere spared me. For a long time, I cursed them for it."

"Now I'll help bring the Crestere to answer for the atrocities they've committed. I'm honored to work with a Seer and her companion." She met my eyes.

Her striking beauty and feminine features gave the impression of delicacy, but beneath her pretty exterior there was strength and determination that could be easily underestimated.

I stared into her hazel eyes struggling to find words to express how I felt. She smiled and nodded understanding without words.

Quiet waves of sorrow pooled around Simon.

"Simon?" I asked, wondering what prompted the sudden outpouring from him.

"Aye, Sweetness?" His eyes locked with mine. His emotional energy rushed over my skin, cool and heavy—deep sympathy. He was familiar with Kali's story.

"Never mind." I shifted in my seat and peered out the window.

The Colorado landscape was breathtaking. A gradual merging of rolling hills crashed into jutting snow-capped mountains heading west. The sun set on the horizon, creating an explosion of pink and orange that lit up the sky. The colors reminded me of the imprint color on Jenny's bracelet. I checked my phone again—nothing.

I glanced at Adric.

He looked like a different person than the man I'd kissed at the house. Tracker Adric was focused and lethal. Dressed from head to toe in black tactical gear, his huge body, which I'd come to think of as a shelter, seemed more like a menacing storm on the verge of eruption.

"Jo! Mallie Mary, Cheekyprawn! Shat! Network failed! What kind of backwoods mompie kind of place are we in? I can't get a bloody signal! Shat! Shat! Shat!" Simon closed his laptop with a snap.

I laughed. Adric and Kali joined in. "What language is that?" I could barely get the words out in between bursts of laughter. I snorted, producing further hysterics.

"Simonese," Adric added.

Beo joined in and yodeled a crooning howl.

Simon joined in. "That bloody beast is either a complete domkop or brilliant—a laughing wolf."

The idea our success hinged on both our ability to find Cyrus and my ability to read a sociopathic mastermind, yet escape his grasp, was equally as laughable as Simon's incomprehensible South African slang. The thought must have dawned on us all at the same time because the car was suddenly silent.

Adric exited at Morrison Road and pulled into a filling station. I stayed in the car, trying to decide if getting out for fresh air or staying as still as possible was better for my growing anxiety.

Adric leaned against the car and allowed the open driver side door to usher in fresh night air. Simon and Kali also stood outside. It looked a lot like an unofficial S.W.A.T. team guarding a foreign dignitary. The fact that Adric insisted we dress like military personnel in order to collect information didn't help to calm my nerves. I moved to open my door.

My phone vibrated.

Jenny's picture lit up the screen. "Jenny!" There was silence on the other end. "Jen? Hello?"

An image of a skeletal-thin blond man standing at the doors of a concrete building flashed in my mind. I leaned back in my seat, struck by the image. He radiated hatred. My body recoiled in a rush of panic as he pushed open the doors of the building and a heavy purple fog poured out followed by Jenny's screams.

I blinked.

"Jenny! Jenny!" I was roaring into the phone like a maniac. Adric took the phone. "No! What are you doing? Give it back! Something's wrong!" He tossed the phone through the air to Simon.

"Trace it." Adric barked the command before looking at me. "What did you see?"

"No! I have to talk to her! Give it back!" Adric clasped my shoulders and held me inches from his face. He shook me several times. The jarring was infuriating. I wanted to slap him, but he had my arms trapped.

"Ione! What did you see?"

"Let go!" I demanded.

"Shut up and listen to me!" His deep voice thrown in my face with force snapped me out of my hysterics. "What did you see?"

I finally heard him.

"What does Cyrus Reid look like?" In all the time we'd spent talking about the Crestere, I'd never thought to ask to see his picture. "Ghostly thin with pale skin?" I met Adric's eyes.

He nodded, just once—a barely detectable confirmation.

I went limp in Adric's grip. "He has Jenny."

TWENTY-ONE

Simon used a computer program to download information from the call. After a quick game of satellite map reading, he pinpointed the location where the call was placed—a church hidden in the mountains outside Morrison. His description of the building coincided with my vision. I feared we would soon find out whether that was a good or bad thing.

We drove in dark silence, winding back and fourth a switchback mountain road. I shivered when the towering concrete walls of the Red Rocks Free Church were within view. The building was different than in my vision, but the resemblance was enough.

"That's it." I whispered.

Adric maneuvered our vehicle into a hidden spot among the pine trees and sagebrush that blanketed the mountains. We were a good distance from the church. The building was an imposing structure, out of place in the mountains. A large mass of vertical concrete jutted out of the surrounding rocky landscape.

I stepped out of the car and was assaulted by energy. I leaned against the SUV and closed my eyes. There were a large number of Vryzoldak in the area, more than I'd ever been around at one time.

"Ione?" Adric tried to focus my attention.

I opened my eyes and saw a talking blob of shadowy darkness. I laughed.

"Are you all right?" Adric's voice was equal parts concern and annoyance.

My reaction was completely inappropriate. I should've been deathly serious, but the influence of the surrounding energies was drug-like. I was lightheaded and sick. A ball of tension rested in my gut, but I continued to giggle. The fact that I was laughing was confusing.

"I been tellin' 'im he looks goofy for almost a decade." I glanced at Simon—another shapeless blob. I laughed harder.

"I'm glad you're finding some comic relief." Adric wasn't glad. He was pissed off. His anger was obvious without the ability to feel the emotion pulsing from his body. "Are you done?" He waited impatiently for my reply.

I closed my eyes and tried to quiet the throbbing impulses swirling inside my head. "I'm sorry. It's...what's the plan?" I shivered.

"Can you see anything else? Is Cyrus Reid here?" I could see Adric's breath as he spoke, billows of warmth lit up by moonlight in the frozen air.

I closed my eyes and tried to relax. I had no idea what I was searching for. I attempted to ignore the cold and pushed away the invading energies to make room in my head for something else. An image flashed before me.

Blackness came bursting from the building.

I gasped and opened my eyes. "He must be in there."

Adric took a step away. The moonlight didn't allow me to see his face. He was shadow in his motion.

"It's too big a risk."

"What!" Anxiety compounded the already sickly sensations stirring in my gut.

Adric continued. "We don't have any advantage in this setting. The Crestere will outnumber us. That building is likely crawling with them."

I took a step closer to Adric, silently praying he wasn't serious.

"That phone call was an invitation. Cyrus gave us exactly what we needed to find this location."

"Doesn't that seem dangerously suspicious? I don't like it."

"You don't like it? Are you kidding? How do you think Jenny feels?" Adric ignored me. "Damn it, Adric! He knows we're close. He knows *exactly* who and what I am. The attack in the field was supposed to be a capture. Jeremy Hitland didn't expect a fight. He made the mistake of underestimating me. If Cyrus wanted me dead that is exactly what I'd be. He's gone to all the trouble of hunting down the one person who is enough of a lure to get my attention. He wants *me*. *That* is our one and only advantage."

I crossed my arms over my chest and dug my feet into the frozen ground. "If you refuse to help, and Jenny dies in there tonight, I will never forgive you."

"The council didn't send the four of us to take on the entire goddamned Crestere organization." Adric closed the small gap between us. "This is leading a lamb to slaughter."

Simon chimed in. "The council is a bunch of arsemongers, Captain. Kali and myself not included, of course." Simon paused, his form shifting in the darkness. "It's politics. The power of the council and that of the Crestere is a delicate balance. They've no mind of this Jenny woman. It's cowardly, but it's how they operate. She'll be long dead before they send help."

"I can't let her die, Adric. I can't." I dropped my angry front and pleaded with him. "She's all I have left."

174

Adric barked orders. "Kali—Simon and I need fifteen minutes to set up surveillance and review the building blueprints. Simon? You can get them?"

Simon's terse nod was barely perceptible in the dark but enough for Adric.

"I'll ready our weapons. When I give you a signal, Kali, take Ione inside. Request a meeting with Cyrus. You're a senior ranking member of the council. Maybe that'll give formality to the meeting. He has to know Ione is under the council's protection." He paused. "Not that it's much insurance."

I stared into the darkness for several moments as reality crept into my mind.

"What about Beo?" I sounded like I felt—terrified.

"Let him loose. He'll know to stay out of trouble and out of sight."

I opened the hatchback. Beo moved from the vehicle into the woods in silence.

I wanted to follow him into the abyss of the mountains and outpace the danger lurking in the building behind me. I knew I couldn't. Not with Jenny trapped inside with a evil incarnate.

"Kali, you know what to do. Get her in front of Reid. Simon and I will get you out. Ione, I know you're worried about Jenny, but we need proof that'll indisputably convict Cyrus Reid and the Crestere of the murders. Then we can put an end to all of this madness."

I reached out and took his hand. "You'll keep me safe."

"This is a shitty plan." He stepped away. "Are you comfortable carrying a handgun?"

"Um…yeah." He handed me a small 9mm in a belt holster. "I have my knife, too."

I walked back to the vehicle and reached into the small bag I brought with me. The ivory inlay on my small four-inch hunting blade glittered in the moonlight. The skin-tight clothing I was wearing didn't allow for pockets, and I had no way of carrying it on my belt. I slid the closed blade into my sports bra.

I startled at the sound of a quiet whistle from behind us.

Kali touched my arm. "That's our signal. It'll take us awhile to reach the building from here." Her hand moved from my elbow to take my palm in hers. "Remember, Cyrus wants you alive. So do Adric, Simon and I."

TWENTY-TWO

The church was going to swallow me whole. The emotions radiating through the air bordered on paralyzing. My head pounded. I closed my eyes without consciously making the choice. Breathing was difficult.

"Clear out the other energies. Turn everything down in your mind." Kali's voice was a life preserver floating in a sea of nauseating emotions.

I visualized her words. Eventually, I was able to manipulate the emotional currents. My eyes opened.

"Good girl." Kali smiled, and turned to lead us the last hundred feet or so to the edge of the church parking lot.

An abnormally large man appeared before us. I craned my neck to look him in the face. Nerves rolled in my belly.

"Ms. Gupta, how do you do? We weren't expecting a visit from the council." He was definitely expecting us. As his thundering voice filled my ears, my remaining senses flooded with his emotion. Like his body, they were massive and their strength intrusive. The man was Vryzoldak. I swallowed back the anxious energy climbing higher in my throat. "How can I be of assistance?"

He grabbed Kali by the arm before he'd finished his sentence. Several other men surrounded us. Hands were gripping my body and searching for weapons. They took our phones, guns, and the knife Kali stashed in her boot.

No one checked my bra. The cool metal of my small knife against my skin was an answered prayer.

They pushed us into the building through a side door. I hadn't heard Kali ask to see Cyrus, but I was sure that was where they were taking us. The corridor where we stood was darker than the outdoors without the light of the moon. I couldn't see a thing. Another door opened, and we were ushered into what must've been the building's basement.

The emotional atmosphere inside was chillingly cold. The building's walls were throwing a yellow-orange imprint color similar to what I expected to see in a church. It conveyed a sense of warmth in stark contrast to the emotional energy within the building.

One of the goons tightened his grip on my arm. We went through another door, up a short set of stairs, and into a small room.

"Wait here," Kali's escort grumbled.

My arms were released. Blood flow returned to my hands. I stood closer to Kali. The burliest of the men left the room while the other two stood blocking the exit.

I attempted to scope out the emotional environment as far as my sight would stretch. The energy was a jumbled mess. I struggled to separate it into individual streams of energy. One was much stronger than the others—dark, angry, and focused. There was another distinct energy, too. Weak as it was, there was something about it that tugged me. It was an imprint I recognized, but an emotion that felt misplaced.

"Jenny!" The shriek burst out of my throat with urgency, and I moved to the door.

Kali grabbed my shoulders. "Ione! Wait." She caught me in the steady gaze of her golden eyes. "We'll find her, but you must wait."

The big man returned, and we were forced down a short hallway into a larger room. The building was too warm. Smells of body odor, cranked heaters, and dust made the air thick.

We stopped in the doorway to the main sanctuary of the church. Two sections of wooden pews were divided down the middle by a wide aisle. The aisle ended dramatically with huge floor to ceiling windows. Acidic bile rose in my throat. I fought back a building scream.

Jenny was on display—tied, gagged, and hanging naked in a mock-crucified position on a huge wooden cross. A spotlight, providing the only lighting in the room, shone directly on her body. It amplified the texture and colors of her burns. Her head was shaved revealing burns there as well. I jumped when a low, emotionless voice echoed from the shadows behind her.

"Welcome council member Gupta. I see you brought me a gift. How thoughtful. Considering you're showing up in such poor fashion, it does seem appropriate. Tell me, what do you think of my decorations?"

A cry escaped me. I pulled against the men holding me. "Jenny!"

A skeletal man appeared in the spot light. He looked young for the amount of rasp accompanying his voice. I flinched, realizing he was the man from my vision.

"Cyrus, there is no need to play games. Let us be civil, and please, take the girl down. Her suffering is unnecessary." Kali's voice was calm but stern.

I turned my attention to the man now making his way toward us—Cyrus Reid. He wasn't an exact avatar of what I'd seen in my vision. He appeared to be in his late thirties with iridescently light blue eyes.

His long, lean frame was clothed in an expensive suit. His cheeks were hollowed, as was the space at his temples. While it all fit together in an almost attractive way, it had a ghoulish effect. Goose bumps crawled up my skin.

He walked to me, stopping just short of touching his body against mine, and leaned in. I could see a faint hint of black on his breath as he exhaled. He was living, breathing hatred. I flinched. His thin lips parted to show even, white teeth under a haunting grin.

His emotions were heavily guarded. I could read him, but within moments, I realized what I could sense was only what he allowed me to read. He continued standing too close. His excitement made my head spin. I glanced past him at Jenny, forcing my mind to focus on why I'd come in the first place.

"She has nothing to do with this. If you took her to get at me, you have me. Let her go." My voice trembled. I tried to avoid looking into his eyes.

His aura of malice pushed against me. He enjoyed making me uncomfortable. It further fueled his excitement. I resisted the urge to back away just to spite him.

He leaned in to kiss me. I closed my eyes, trying not to anticipate the sensation of his vile lips on mine. His mouth hovered before he turned away, bringing his lips to my ear instead.

"What do you see?" As he said it, he unleashed his full intention.

I was slammed with images.

Cyrus planned to lead the Crestere on a death march, killing all who didn't adhere to his will. He was using the Juice. The drug Dr. Mullins had used to heal me, Cyrus was using to control and kill. He was capturing Vryzoldak, drugging them and extracting blood plasma to replenish his supply. There would be another attack tonight. He was holding a group in a nearby room. Dozens would die.

The visions came in quick flashes, and with them, an entire spectrum of emotions from Cyrus, the other Crestere members, and the captives. I choked out loud as my body shook with a low volt of electricity. The men holding me stepped away. I gasped for air and fell to the ground.

Cyrus caught me in his gaze. He'd allowed me to see his plans, and he was acutely aware of my reaction. Something in the way his emotion felt was different. His energy was a live wire. Vryzoldak energy was overpowering, Pharmak power subtle, but he was a downed power line—dangerous, unruly, and deadly.

He turned, leaving me alone on the floor, and walked to Jenny. He was too powerful. I frantically searched for Adric and Simon. There was no indication they were anywhere close. Fear and hopelessness washed over me. My breathing doubled, my heart raced, and my vision narrowed. I fought against the panic threatening to take me under.

Kali reached for my hand and pulled me to my feet. The contact was calming. It reminded me of what she'd said as we'd approached the building. I focused. We wouldn't make it out of this mess, but I would *not* allow Cyrus Reid the pleasure of knowing he could undo me so easily. If nothing else, I owed it to Jenny to defy him in any way I could.

He stood just below Jenny. Her head lulled to one side as a barely audible moan escaped her gag. She was on the verge of total unconsciousness. Tears ran down my cheeks. What had I done getting her mixed up in this?

"Jenny, I'm sorry." There was no way of knowing if she'd heard me.

Cyrus turned to face us and raised his hands in the air. Lights illuminated the room. It remained dim, but I was now able to see the entire sanctuary. More Crestere members had gathered around us. Kali huddled closer.

Again, I scanned, checking for any sign of Adric or Simon, reaching for their energy. I thought of Beo, terrified someone would catch him, and Cyrus would torture him along with the rest of us.

There was no sign of any of them.

"We are gathered here to mark the turning of an age. We have made such progress." Cyrus stared at me. "Gone will be the days of hiding, pretending, and subservience. Now we take what is owed to our people. For too long we've bent in submission to a weaker race. A leadership that would have us believe we are *not* a chosen people has taught us a false doctrine. We are the chosen tribe, and we will rally against those who try to maintain their own power by teaching us to fear ourselves."

Cyrus's voice reached a fever pitch, and the energy he was generating brushed against my skin. Gooseflesh crawled up my arms. The emotional energy in the room hummed with excitement. He bowed his head before continuing.

"Tonight it truly begins. No one can deny our strength after what we've shown in these past weeks. After tonight, we will be known openly and respected rightfully."

The crowd applauded. Cyrus stood arms outstretched, soaking in the approval.

"Let us begin." With his final words, Cyrus's eyes met mine. He unleashed another flash of his intention.

Jenny would be killed first—an example of inferior weakness. Those he'd captured and were drugged—semi-comatose somewhere in the church. They would follow.

"No!" My shout came out sounding less like the authoritative command I'd meant and more like a plea. I took several steps toward the stage. Cyrus held up a hand to quiet the crowd and nodded for me to speak.

"Take me. Release Jenny and Kali and the others you're holding here. If you allow them all to leave safely, I'll stay. You have what you want."

Cyrus's face broke out in an amused smile. The effect was chilling. "I'm not sure I like your tone.

Giving orders is not the wisest choice for someone in your situation. Perhaps, you aren't as valuable as you'd have me believe if you can't *see* where this is going." He laughed.

I brought my hand to my chest and quickly gripped my switchblade. I snapped open the knife and held it at the base of my throat just beneath my jawline. It bounced in time with my hammering heartbeat. I forced the knife though my skin deep enough to draw a trickle of blood. My hand shook.

Tears continued to fall from my eyes as I kept them trained on Cyrus. He gave nothing away except a barely noticeable flare of his nostrils.

His voice was stoic and detached. "You aren't the killing kind. But please, go ahead, run yourself through." Cyrus nodded at the goons closest to me, an unsaid order to detain me.

I pushed the knife harder. Pain exploded with radiating heat where the knife pressed into my skin. The slow trickle of blood became a stream. Warmth spread across my chest as blood soaked into the fabric of my clothes.

Cyrus nodded, and the men stopped.

"Ione, no." Kali's voice trembled.

I ignored her. "I've nothing to lose, Cyrus. If you kill her and the others you're hiding, I won't have their blood on my hands. I'll die first." The words were gritted out between my clenched teeth.

What began as a desperate act was no longer just a stunt. I was prepared to cut my own throat, and Cyrus Reid knew it.

"Untie the girl and take her down." Cyrus spoke just above a whisper, but whomever he was speaking to heard him. Instantaneously, Jenny was being lowered from the cross. "Put the knife down." He was no longer whispering. He said each word with slow direction and in a tone that brought the temperature in the room down another ten degrees.

I didn't move.

"Ione." Jenny's voice was weak, but I'd heard it. I momentarily took my eyes from Cyrus to look at her.

All it took was a single moment of distraction.

Someone gripped my wrists, tore the knife from my hand, and held my arms tight behind my back. I grunted in pain as my hands were bound.

I glanced up to see Cyrus standing in front of me. I took a step back and a large, hard body filled the space behind me.

Cyrus closed the remaining inches between us, holding his face close to mine. Our bodies were strangely similar in shape and size. My body ached with the desire to escape our close proximity. He stood closer, bringing his whole body next to mine. His hands clasped my arms above where they were bound. He may have been a thin, wiry man, but he was incredibly strong, judging from the inescapable hold he had on me.

I looked to the stage again in search of Jenny. She'd balled herself into a fetal position, still naked, but with the gag and ties removed. She seemed on the verge of death. Panic shot through me. I twisted my head to see Cyrus.

"Let Kali take her out of here. Let them go." I'd lost all bargaining force. I was begging. "Please. Please let her go."

It aroused him to watch me beg. His pleasure was a slimy emotion, moist and clammy as it flowed across my skin. I twitched at the sensation and closed my eyes, trying to maintain my control over the energies in the room.

I was struck again with the heady charge of his emotions. I was zapped with the low-voltage shock of his desire to watch suffering. He was going to kill Jenny—slowly. His desire to do so was so strongly connected to his emotional energy; he may as well have said the words.

Frantic panic rolled through me. I clawed at his emotions with my sight and pushed against his walls. I dug at his barriers, pulling at his black heart. It wasn't enough. I drew on all the emotional forces I'd previously worked so hard to quiet. I reached out into the room, gathered any and all I could grasp within the church. Pulling the energies together was no different than holding lit explosives in my bare hands. They snapped and popped, sending unpredictable and surprising shocks through my body.

Directing that quantity of emotional energy was vastly different than the bending I'd done before. My body stiffened with electrical current. My chest was ready to burst, my head throbbed, and my vision blurred. I thrust the energy at Cyrus.

I poured all I could gather into his body through our points of contact. Cyrus's grip tightened. He gasped for air as he fell to his knees. His body stiffened, but his hands remained glued to me acting as conductors to my current.

His eyes pleaded to make it stop. I pushed harder. My hair stood on end as the electric-like current coursed through us. Lights flickered, and electrical fires spontaneously ignited at power sources throughout the room.

I could hear shouts and screams. Smoke filled the church. A gun went off, more screams, another gunshot. Heat surged though my body. The sickening scent of burning hair filled my lungs.

"I have her, Ione!" Kali's voice came from the direction of the stage. In my peripheral vision, I could see her cradling Jenny in her arms. A man standing near the stage drew a gun and pointed it at Kali.

"Kali!" I heard Simon's voice, a shout of urgent warning.

The weight of Cyrus's body pulled on mine, twisting me in his grip.

More guns fired, and the emotional current became stronger as panic rose. My hands and feet scorched with pain.

"Ione! Stop! It's too strong!" Adric's voice bellowed in the sanctuary. "It's burning you!"

His words settled into my mind. I howled, realizing the stench of burning hair and skin was my own body reacting to electrocution. I crumpled onto the ground and fought the overwhelming urge to pass out.

The energy was gone, and with it, my ability to overpower Cyrus.

TWENTY-THREE

"Nathaniel!" Cyrus's voice overpowered the ringing in my ears.

People ran back and forth—more shouting and gunshots. Cyrus slammed me against a wall. The only advantage to the exhaustion taking over my body was a dulled sensation to pain.

"Nathaniel!" Cyrus shouted again.

A man appeared, dressed in tactical gear.

"Yes, sir." Light hazel eyes offset skin only a few shades lighter than his dark clothing. He was built like a fighter—strong but lithe. He waited for instructions, impervious to the chaos around us.

"I want Adric Silverman dead!" Cyrus shouted, spittle spraying down his chin.

"We're in pursuit, sir. Only a matter of time."

"Simon Brown and Kali Gupta? They're Council. Keep them alive."

"Sir, it may be too late. Josiah's shot went though the head."

"What? How did that happen?" Cyrus's voice was demanding. Fury wafted off him, stinging my senses.

"Sir, while you were…injured." He paused. "Gupta, went for the girl. Josiah fired. Brown took the girl and escaped."

I twisted in Cyrus's grip. I could make out the front of the church. Kali's body lay on the floor. Simon and Jenny were gone.

I threw myself in the direction of the stage. "No! Kali!" My voice sounded strangled. Cyrus gripped my arms and pressed me against the wall.

"Can you get us out of here?" He asked Nathaniel with impatience.

Nathaniel nodded.

Cyrus bent down, jutting his shoulder into my stomach, and threw me over his body. I swallowed a gaping breath as pain exploded in my abdomen. I choked on the smell of scorched hair and skin. A wave of fear tormented my body when I imagined what would soon be the gaping holes and black, rotting flesh of electrical burns covering my hands and feet.

Heavy exhaustion settled in weighing down my eyelids. I bounced and bobbed like a rag doll.

Freezing air assaulted my bare skin as Cyrus stepped outside. I let out a moan through gritted teeth.

"Shut up!" Cyrus's voice dripped with anger.

Three bullets whizzed by us, whistling rockets of lead. Nathaniel returned fire.

"Silverman." His voice was even and calm—more like he was answering the phone than informing Cyrus who was firing at us.

"Silverman! I'll kill her!" Cyrus bellowed the threat into the night as he dropped us both to the ground and dragged me through the dirt of the parking lot.

"Adric!" My voice was weak as it scratched inside my throat.

Nathaniel hoisted me into the rear passenger side seat of a boxy SUV. Cyrus crawled in beside me. Nathanial was instantly in the driver's seat, furiously driving down the mountain. I started to sense the last of my energy seeping from my body. God only knew where I might wake up if I passed out.

I reached out to Cyrus with my sight. He tensed as I dug in his head. Something wasn't right. A sting zapped my eyes, and I flexed against the pain. Cyrus lurched toward me, grabbing my throat.

"Do not push me." His grip tightened. "Stay out of my head. Do you understand?"

I fought for air.

Cyrus released my throat and returned to his seat. I could tell he was in pain, but far less than me.

I had nothing left. If I could endure the pain and read Cyrus, he'd know I was there. The aching in my body intensified. I knew what was coming. I had only a few minutes of consciousness.

"Why?" I asked, in a scratchy whisper.

Inside the vehicle was dark, what light existed, reflected off Cyrus's eyes as he fixed them on me.

"That stunt you attempted was more impressive than you know. There's only one line of Seers with that kind of ability. You're a Kreefos—as I suspected. I should thank you for proving it so quickly." His voice was harsh, and the rasp echoed in my head. "It goes against my personal policy, of course, but you're worth more to me alive than dead."

I stared at him. His words shot a hot spike of adrenaline through my veins. "You sadistic bastard! What is it you want from me?" Raw pain scorched my throat as I squeezed out every syllable.

He leaned in close. "Don't you know?" The tangy smell of his breath mingled with the acrid stench of my burns. My mouth watered—a precursor to vomit.

I spat in his face. The sticky saliva hit him in the eyes and he flinched. I catapulted into the front of the car. Cyrus yelled as he reached for me. He grabbed the fabric of my pants, and the sound of the material tearing filled the car. By some miracle, amid the flailing the bind that held my hands together loosened enough for one of my hands to escape. I grabbed frantically at the passenger unlock button and the door handle.

Nathaniel yanked the wheel and slammed on the breaks. I lost my grip on the door. My head ricocheted off the dash. Strong hands gripped my legs, holding me down. I screamed and kicked while reaching for the door.

The sound of shattering glass exploded in my ears. The hands restraining my legs released. I heard gunshots. Broken glass sprinkled across my back and legs—the door opened.

"No!" I heard Cyrus's gravely voice.

I pulled my body into the passenger seat. Cyrus clenched a fistful of my ponytail in his hand. My body fell out the door while my head remained fixed in his grip. I bawled out in pain. My cry was matched with a roar from Cyrus.

Warm liquid ran down my forehead into my eyes. Cyrus's grip released. I tumbled out of the car, hitting the ground with a thud.

"Run!" Adric's voice thundered.

Bullets flew from every direction. I could hear garbled yells from both Adric and Nathaniel. Cyrus continued roaring in pain. I blinked the blood out of my eyes and crawled up the embankment of the road. When I hit the tree line, I stood and ran.

Pain seared through my burned feet. I sucked in air, desperate to keep moving and stay conscious as blackness threatened to overtake me.

TWENTY-FOUR

I jolted awake and searched the darkness, trying to place myself. I felt a familiar nudge. Beo prodded my body with his nose.

The relief of seeing him brought tears to my eyes. I grabbed the scruff of his neck. Pain radiated in my hands. I moaned. Beo whined and licked my face before prodding me again. He was trying to get me moving. I forced myself up to my aching feet.

The frosty air helped sharpen my senses but assaulted my body. I trembled with cold and pain but followed Beo's form through he moonlit woods.

Beo stopped. I heard the click of a gun safety.

"Stop." Adric's voice echoed in the darkness.

Relief washed over my body. "Adric!"

"Thank God." His voice came from my right.

Beo walked toward Adric's voice. I stumbled behind. My eyes made out his shape propped against a tree.

"Over here," he said. I couldn't read his emotions. Using my second sight felt like touching numb skin.

I bent down and steadied myself with my hands against his shoulders before falling into him.

"How badly are you hurt?" Adric's hands were on me, feeling my arms and working their way up to my shoulders.

"My hands and feet—I'm not sure what I did to Cyrus in the church, but it caused electrical burns." He touched my hands sending pain radiating through my arms.

"What about your neck?"

The tender spot below my jawline throbbed. "I don't know. I think it stopped bleeding."

"We need to get out of here." I watched as his head fall back resting on the tree behind him. Fear curdled in my belly.

"How long has it been since I ran from the car?" I asked.

"A few hours at most." He glanced to the eastern horizon where the first signs of light were beginning to flirt with the night.

"Did you kill Cyrus?"

"One bullet to the hand and one to the shoulder won't kill him. Nathaniel managed to get him back into the car. After I was shot, they took off—"

"What! Shot? Where?" I sat up.

"My leg. I'll be fine, but I'm slow. It's going to take time to get out of here." For the first time, I was grateful to hear his clipped, professional tone.

"Tell me what you need me to do." I attempted to match his voice.

"The vehicle is fairly close. We need to get there. Then we find a doctor."

It wasn't the detailed plan I'd been hoping for. He didn't have someone waiting for us. I slouched against him.

"What have I done?" My voice cracked, sounding as broken as my body.

Adric wrapped me in his arms melting me with his warmth.

"Shhh." He ran his fingers over my hair. "You told us enough to know he had people there he was planning to kill. They were locked in a room in the basement—drugged out of their minds. We did get them out." I turned to see Adric. "Simon has Jenny. We'll find them both."

He ran his hand along one side of my face. His eyes searched mine for something. "What else did you see, Ione?"

I swallowed. "He's living, breathing hatred." I shivered. "He's using Juice—both to control and to kill. He's harvesting it from the Vryzoldak he's holds

197

prisoner." I swallowed again. "He wants me alive. He wants to use me for something, but I don't know what." My entire body trembled. Adric pulled me closer.

I rested my head against his broad chest and forced my racing heart to meet the steady beat of his. "He said I'm a Kreefos. My genetic line has something to do with why he wants me." The thought made my stomach lurch. "Adric…he's terrifying." My lungs restricted. "Kali."

"Kali knew the risks involved before she volunteered." His arms loosened their hold, and he shifted our bodies, tilting my head back. He brushed my hair from my grime-covered face. His fingers gently wiped away my tears. "We need to go now."

After an hour of walking, the sun broke over the horizon and made maneuvering through the mountainside easier. Unfortunately, it did nothing to ease the horrific pain pulsing through my body. Adric did what he could to help me, supporting me as we made our way through the woods, but his body was nearly as thrashed as mine. The bullet wound in his leg stopped bleeding thanks to a makeshift tourniquet. His clothes were torn in various places, and he was covered in small scratches and scrapes.

We were more or less following Beo. Why we settled on that plan wasn't something we discussed. I figured if he was going in the wrong direction Adric would know. I didn't have the energy to contemplate our heading.

"We've got to be close." Adric grunted out the words between steps taken with his injured leg.

"God, I hope so." At elevation, the air was frigid. The wind picked up, and the low temperatures bit at my skin. I didn't know if the growing pain in my hands and feet was due to the electrical burns or frostbite. Either way, they were going to start turning shades of blue and purple soon.

"There it is," Adric whispered.

I squinted and made out the shape of our SUV. Adric put his hand on my arm, and I stopped. He put one finger over his mouth and pulled out a gun with his other hand.

Beo glanced back at me before silently making his way through the trees to the car. Adric pulled my body close to his and brought us both into the shadow of the nearby trees. He watched as Beo made his way to the vehicle—the self-appointed scout. After several minutes of sniffing the area, Beo stood waiting.

"Let's go. Quiet—and stay close."

The short walk to the car seemed longer than the hour we'd been wandering the woods. Adric dug under the chassis of the SUV and pulled out a set of keys.

"Get in."

The moment the door unlocked, I crawled in locking the door behind me with a bruised elbow.

Adric let Beo into the car and took his place in the driver's seat. "Let's get the hell out of here."

TWENTY-FIVE

"I need to take her home." I didn't like talking to Alexander Odin, but after facing Cyrus Reid, this conversation barely qualified as uncomfortable.

"My dear, I realize you believe it is in her best interest she be escorted home by no one other than yourself. However, I believe you fail to see the risk such a situation may pose."

"You can't keep her here forever. She has a family—a life, and she wants to go home."

"Ms. McCreery, are you speaking about your friend, or are you, perhaps, speaking of your own desires?" Alexander's graceful movements were hypnotic as he paced his office.

I was thankful he was guarded. My sight wasn't back to normal, and reading emotions caused excruciating headaches. I glanced down to avoid eye contact and focused on my perfectly healed hands.

Taking Juice the second time was far more difficult. I tried to staunch the shudder that ran through my body.

"I've already agreed to help the council in any way I can. I appreciate all you've done for me and for Jenny. I know we had Dr. Mullins' help because of you. Her body is better, but *she* isn't. And she won't be until she can go home. No disrespect, Minister, but I don't trust anyone else to take her."

"No one?" Alexander raised one perfectly arched eyebrow.

"Adric and Simon are going with me."

"Yes, I heard." He leaned against his desk. "You are quite the puzzle, Ms. McCreery."

Something in his voice was setting off alarm bells in my head. His dark, abyss-like eyes held me in his gaze. The last time he'd done that, he'd unleashed a torrent of emotion that sent me into seizure.

"A lot has changed in the last few weeks." I leaned in closer, intent on holding his stare. "The thing is, I came here as a courtesy. You're the council leader, and I thought it appropriate to tell you I planned to take Jenny home. I've already arranged for what help I need—and like I said, I'll come back."

I stood, closing what was left of the space between us. "Mr. Odin, you and I both know the stories circulating about me aren't accurate, but I scare the shit out of almost everyone in this place. You may be council head, but if I take this to them, they'll agree to let me go and likely tell me not to let the door hit me on the way out."

I felt the urge to dig inside his head and discover what was going on there. I swallowed it back, knowing it would only cause me pain.

A grin tugged at the corners of Alexander's mouth, but the sentiment didn't reach his eyes. "A puzzle, indeed." He stood, and I took a step back. "Very well." He made his way to his chair. "If you don't return in three days time, I'll send for you."

I couldn't hold back the snort of disgust that escaped my throat. "I said I'd be back. If not because I keep my word, then because nothing will keep me from attending Kali's funeral."

"Ms. McCreery, this situation is about to change dramatically. It won't take long for us to finish making arrangements with our people in law enforcement. When the council votes in favor of an official criminal investigation and sanctioned pursuit of the Crestere…" he paused. "It wouldn't be an exaggeration to describe what's to come as war. It'll be dangerous for someone like you to be…" he hesitated again, "…without strong allies."

Alexander Odin was not as terrifying as Cyrus Reid, but there was no doubt in my mind he was cut from the same cloth. "Allies would've been handy when we took on the entire Crestere to save Jenny and the dozens of Vryzoldak set to die."

Alexander ignored my dig. Jenny was no one to the council. Had I known Cyrus was keeping thirty Vryzoldak hostages before we entered the church, they would've sent help. While that sounded like a justifiable explanation to Alexander, I thought it was complete horseshit. I reminded him at every opportunity.

The door to the office opened, and Adric stepped in. He looked strong despite the limp in his walk. He'd refused to take any Juice, insisting his wound would heal fast enough on its own.

"Three days, Adric." Alexander's voice was authoritative.

Adric reached out and put a hand on the small of my back. "We'll be back." Adric kept his eyes on Alexander, but his words were also directed at me. Left up to him, I'd stay behind under lock and key in the depths of Alexander's Chicago mansion guarded by fifty heavily armed Vryzoldak.

Truth be told, I was satisfied to stay at the mansion where I could keep alive the delusion we were safe, but Jenny made it clear she wanted to go home. I couldn't send her with strangers, not after what she'd been through, and not knowing Cyrus was still alive.

We would take Jenny to her grandparents' home in northern Wyoming. Their ranch was as secluded a place as existed. No one strange or unknown would find it without being seen by one of the locals.

"Ione?" Adric stepped toward the door, leaving his hand outstretched to me.

I put my hand in his and interlaced our fingers. My body fell in step with his. All the fears I had about Cyrus Reid and the Crestere, about getting Jenny back home safely, about what was waiting for me when the council mounted an official attack—it all vanished.

I knew the feeling wouldn't last, but the comfort was compelling. I heard Alexander's office door click closed. I stopped. Adric nudged me against the wall and pressed his lips to mine. He pulled away, creating only enough space to speak.

"We'll leave within the hour."

I closed my eyes and pulled in his scent. I was still riding the high of the Juice. I rested my face against his chest.

"We found Cyrus. We did what we were supposed to do. By some miracle, Jenny's alive. We saved people. This should be the end." I swallowed back the bitterness rising in my throat. "It's just the beginning."

"Did you see something?"

I shook my head. His embrace was intoxicating as it mingled with his scent. "No one is ever really safe."

He loosened his grasp. "Well, what do you suggest? Oh, wise Seer," he smirked.

I laughed halfheartedly. "Someone told me once, you don't have to forget or pretend, but you do have try for some kind of normal life." I smiled thinking of Jenny. "I don't know what normal is anymore, but I've tried hiding—maybe it felt safe, but it wasn't living. This—" I pressed my lips to his, "—this, is living. And it's worth fighting for."

ABOUT THE AUTHOR

JANSEN CURRY is a multi-genre writer. She is also the author and creator of the blog, The Tall Mom (www.thetallmom.com).

She makes her home in the beautifully under-populated state of Wyoming with her husband, three children, and two spoiled rotten Rhodesian Ridgebacks.

27892948R00135

Made in the USA
San Bernardino, CA
17 December 2015